I0451282

THE SILVERSTONE SAGA BOOK 1

ROSEWOOD DREAMS

ABBY FARNSWORTH

This is a work of fiction. Names, characters, places, and incidents are products of the author's imagination or are used fictitiously and are not to be construed as real. Any resemblance to actual events, locations, organizations, or persons, living or dead, is entirely coincidental.

World Castle Publishing, LLC
Pensacola, Florida
Copyright © Abby Farnsworth 2023
Hardback ISBN: 9798375713274
Paperback ISBN: 9781960076281
eBook ISBN: 9781960076298
First Edition World Castle Publishing, LLC, February 14, 2023
http://www.worldcastlepublishing.com
Licensing Notes
All rights reserved. No part of this book may be used or reproduced in any manner whatsoever without written permission, except in the case of brief quotations embodied in articles and reviews.
Cover: Cover Designs by Karen
Editor: Maxine Bringenberg

Table of Contents

ACKNOWLEDGMENTS

As always, a huge thank you to Karen Fuller, Maxine Bringenberg, and World Castle Publishing. I am beyond thankful for you! Also, thank you to J&M Books and Play, and The Watering Can Art Studio. You guys are great! Thank you to my family and friends for supporting me, as well as Eric Little for hosting so many radio interviews. I appreciate all of you!

Thank you to all of my readers. To those who have left great ratings and reviews, thank you. It is very much appreciated. You have no idea how glad I am that you enjoy my books. You give me extra smiles.

To my *EverGreen Trilogy* readers, thank you for coming back. I'm really glad you decided to join me on another journey! I hope you find this one just as thrilling as the last.

To my *The Shades of Us Trilogy* readers, thank you for deciding to read another one of my books. It's so exciting to share another story with you! I hope you enjoy my new cast of characters.

DEDICATION

To Nicole
All I can say is a simple, "Thank you."

"'Hope' is the thing with feathers -
That perches in the soul -
And sings the tune without the words -
And never stops - at all -"

"'Hope' is the thing with feathers" by Emily Dickinson

PROLOGUE
CASSANDRA

The fire was swarming around me like a herd of monsters ready to devour their prey. Flames jumped up to catch my dress and skin within their hot grasp. Every cell in my body was burning with the sensation of overwhelming heat. Even my red hair couldn't seem to escape the inevitable scorch of this terrible nightmare.

We were burning, literally burning. Constantine was lying beside me with his hands in my hair. He had always loved my red mane. His fingers were tangled in my ruby locks as if the curls were the only thing he could grasp. We knew we were dying. The smoke had already rendered us unable to move. These last few glances were our only attempt at a goodbye. We had these stolen moments to relish in the memory of each other's arms. The fire was growing close enough to completely overtake us. But we had these glimpses, the gentle ones where our eyes met in acknowledgment. We knew it was all coming to a close. Our lives were over. Our marriage had been complicated, but I loved him more than I loved myself. My feelings for him were uncontrollable, and I couldn't have predicted their evolution. It hadn't been a choice. It had just evolved into a love that consumed my heart.

Clovis's hand was touching mine. I could feel his fingers brushing against my own heated skin. We were breathing in sync, so much so that it seemed like our bodies were molding into one. My stomach tightened at his touch. It was fitting and a slightly disturbingly romantic way for me to die. I was lying between two brothers I loved. One was my husband, and the other, my former lover. Energy was pulsing between us as we lay on the floor of our burning home.

My throat continued to tighten as the smoke surrounded us. Constantine's breath was coming out in choked sobs. I was too weak to do any magic. I wanted to save them, to help both of them escape, but I couldn't even muster the strength to move my hands. My lungs were filled with toxic air. We were finished. There was no way we would make it out of this fire alive. We would die just as we had lived, by each others' sides.

I wanted to kiss Constantine one last time and lay my head against his chest as I drifted off into the world of darkness. My fingers yearned for one more touch of Clovis's hand. Just one last time, I wanted to feel their energy again. Just the simple flow of magic between our fingertips would have been enough, but I didn't have much to give. All I had were the teardrops dripping from my eyes. They tumbled down my cheeks to land upon the wooden floor, mingling with the flames.

Outside, I could hear their cheers. The townspeople had discovered us. At first, they had called us heretics and pushed us from society. We hadn't retaliated — there wasn't any reason to. My coven had been content to live separately from the humans. Witches and warlocks were hated among the townspeople. They saw us as evil, not worthy of respect or value. We had left them and lived in the wilderness, a peaceful little life we had created for ourselves. I certainly didn't mind the freedom. We could practice our magic without the fear of judgment or violence.

But apparently, our separation hadn't been enough for them. They wanted to watch us burn. I had heard of the witch trials. They had spread throughout America only twenty years earlier. I had never expected it to happen to us, though. No one ever predicted a tragedy occurring so close to home. There were whispers throughout the magical world that I was the most powerful witch in existence. The townspeople probably didn't know. They weren't involved in witch business. But I was the coven's leader, and I had failed my people. They were all dead.

My baby was gone. I had tried to save her, but the nursery had collapsed. The house was falling down around us. At least she hadn't been in pain — I didn't want her to feel the burning. She had only spent a few precious months in my arms, and now she was gone. Maybe she had been asleep. I could at least pretend that's how it had ended—maybe it would give me a little peace.

"Cassandra," Constantine whispered in a choked voice.

"Yes?" I answered.

"I love you," he mumbled.

I felt the tears continue to drip. "I love you, too."

I glanced over to look at Clovis. I had hoped to say goodbye, but it was too late. I could sense that his heart had stopped. Clovis was gone, and I hadn't had the moment to take one last look. There were things he still needed to know, old feelings I still held. They would die with me now, just as every little whisper of love between us had.

This was the end of us. I didn't want to say goodbye. I'd barely experienced the world, no less all the beautiful aspects of life. I had only been alive for nineteen years. Even so, I had run out of time. The air seemed to be thinning as the smoke smothered my lungs. I tried to keep my eyes open, but I couldn't. My lids became heavy, and my heartbeat erratic. With one final breath, I closed my eyes.

CHAPTER ONE
ESME
MEET AGAIN

The berries I wanted weren't anywhere to be found. I'd already collected the herbs we needed, but the remainder of the ingredients seemed absent from where I usually found them. This section of the woods, only a little way from our village, usually had everything I needed to make a basic healing medication. One of the older women in our coven had contracted some sort of stomach bug, so Marilyn, my best friend, and I had decided to try to make something to help with the pain. I had come to the woods in search of the ingredients but wasn't having very much luck finding them. Perhaps we would have to send someone to the nearest town in search of human medicine. We never liked to do it. Our history with humans was too complicated. But it was the twenty-first century, and they probably wouldn't chase after us with torches and rope. If we needed to venture out to get some of that human medicine packed with some sort of strange, man-made drugs, then we would. Barely anyone seemed to know what was actually in it, but at least it took the pain away.

My basket was overflowing with herbs, but they wouldn't do much good on their own. I had already been wandering around for hours. Maybe it was time to go back and surrender to the inevitability of a trip into the human world. I sighed in exasperation, but just as I was about to turn around, I heard footsteps. A chill went up through my stomach to my heart. I had always had a strange sort of anxiety when it came to strangers. No one really knew why. I'd been born with anxiety in my DNA, and even I didn't understand it. My brain probably just had strange wiring.

I turned around, half expecting to see a deer, but was met with a sight that sent a shock through my body. Two men were standing before me, wearing waterproof clothing and sturdy hiking boots. The first was tall, with a full beard and dark brown curly hair that fell to his shoulders. His chest was wide and sturdy, and his jaw was set in a firm line. When his blue eyes met mine, his mouth opened into a little smile. My breath caught in my throat as our eye contact continued. My jungle, forest-green eyes collided with his frosty-blue ones in a moment that seemed to speak a thousand words. It was as if my heart was thumping against my chest and might burst through my body at any second. I could tell he was stunned, too. I had never seen such a captivating man. Somehow, I wanted to run into his arms and tuck my head against his shoulder. He was taller than me, so much so that his chest was level with my chin. My magic seemed to pulse inside me. He was a warlock, and I could feel his strong, masculine energy flowing out of his body.

Beside him stood another man with dark blond hair that looked like hay on a warm summer day. It was tied in a ponytail behind his head that fell just below his shoulders. He didn't have a full beard, but the shadow of a potential one was clearly evident upon his face. I couldn't pull my eyes away from his gentle lips. They were thick and drew my attention as powerfully as any love spell ever could. A small coil of heat erupted within my abdomen. I could feel his magic, too. They were similar in a way that showed their tie. They were brothers. That much was obvious. The second was slightly shorter than the other with a leaner build, but he was still strong. The muscles in his arms were clearly defined and more than a little toned.

I couldn't tell which of the two I was more drawn to. They both created a warm feeling in my stomach that made me a little sick. I felt nervous in my brown dress and boots as their eyes seemed to travel over me. My red hair fell down my shoulders in a mess of waves that were frizzy from the persistent wind. I knew I wasn't particularly beautiful. I never had been anything out of the ordinary. Average, but not gorgeous. Yet even in the presence of my stunningly normal appearance, they seemed to be incapable of speech.

My chest suddenly felt too big, my stomach too soft, and my thighs too wide. My stubby nails pressed into my palms as we stood in silence. I was seventeen, but I had never looked at a man like I was examining these two. The first was maybe twenty-one, the second perhaps nineteen. My heart was pulsing, something inside me was swooning, and my mind seemed clouded with some sort of emotion I didn't understand.

"Who are you?" I whispered.

"I'm Sampson Silverstone," the first one replied.

His voice was deep and silky. It was so overwhelming I barely processed his words. I wanted to taste the way his name flowed from his tongue. Like a warm tea that traveled down my throat, his voice made my chest expand.

"Everest," the second one added.

He gave me a soft smile and inclined his head slightly. I blushed at his chivalry. He was sweet, more so than I had expected. I gave him a gentle smile in return.

"Esme Brontë," I whispered.

They were both silent for a minute before Sampson spoke. "Are you part of the Black Hills Coven?"

"Yes," I replied.

I was nervous for a moment. But remembering they were warlocks, my anxiety went away. They smiled at me. They'd clearly been looking for us.

"We were hoping to find you," Sampson said. "Our mother recently passed, and we've been looking to join a coven."

I smiled. "Of course! I'd be glad to take you back with me."

My heart gave a little thud as I watched their relieved expressions. They both had sparkling eyes that made my insides feel warm and jumbled. I had never met brothers like this. There was something about them that made my head grow light.

"Thank you," Everest replied.

I glanced up at the sky. The sun was beginning to set. Forgetting all about the berries, I picked up my basket and motioned to the path back to the village. I could hardly believe I had come to the woods in search of ingredients and discovered two incredibly alluring men. How had this happened to me? It was certainly a good day.

"We'd better get going if we want to make it back before dark," I said.

Sampson gave me an excited grin. "Lead the way."

I had never felt so drawn to anyone in my entire life. Their bodies seemed to pull me closer. It seemed as if an incredible amount of energy was flowing between us. I didn't know what to do, but I was certain they felt it too. They smiled as I turned and started walking back home. Marilyn would definitely be surprised at what I brought back from my trip to the woods.

CHAPTER TWO
ESME
TO THE BEGINNING

When we arrived back at the village, it was almost completely dark out. The air was alive with the smell of food, lantern light, and boiling potions. Most people were inside already. I led Sampson and Everest to the little cottage I shared with Marilyn on the outskirts of town.

Never having known our fathers — which was common in our community, as most witches went into the human world to date — we had grown up with our mothers. There were so few warlocks in existence that many witches relied upon human men for reproduction. Of course, this only increased our seemingly unsolvable problem. Magical DNA was different from that of a mortal. Witches could conceive female children from both human and warlock fathers, but the only way to conceive a male child required the father to have magical blood. Simply put, in a community with few warlocks and many witches, almost all the children born were female. No one knew how to solve the issue.

When our population had been plentiful, we'd had almost an even number of both genders. But ever since the legendary massacre of the largest coven in American history, the warlock population had shrunk. Sampson and Everest were the first warlocks around my age I had ever met.

Marilyn and I had both lost our mothers only a few months ago. The human world blamed it on heart disease and breast cancer. Marilyn and I had simply accepted the mortal doctors' explanations. Still, it had been hard. I was only seventeen, and she was barely sixteen. We were best friends, but I also felt I had to take care of her. With no parents, we had to be there for each other.

Our little cottage was made from dark wood, with vines crawling up the sides. The roof was slanted, so it displayed the top of a chimney where smoke was drifting into the night air. The windows were covered with lacy curtains, the color of dusk, and plants surrounded the front door at the end of the stone walkway we were traveling on. My boots thudded softly as my cotton dress blew lightly in the breeze.

As soon as I opened the front door, candlelight enveloped my sight. The smell of fresh bread was everywhere. A small fire was lit in the fireplace, and oils were drifting into the air. Lavender and rose aromas wafted throughout the room. It was a familiar scent. Ever since I was little, we had used such oils for basic skincare and relaxation. They made me feel a sense of comfort that was similar to when I was little.

I had always loved my little refuge, that was our house. The floor was covered in a soft rug that was squishy beneath my feet. There was a large window beside the door with a little bookshelf beneath it. Of course, we had our grimoires — spell books — but we kept other books too. Above the fireplace was a small portrait of Cassandra — she was a legend. She had led the huge coven that had been eradicated shortly after the Salem Witch Trials. As the Greeks kept pictures of Hercules, we held the memory of Cassandra. The portrait was blurry and tainted. Her features were obscured, but it was more about the concept than actually being able to examine her.

There was a large sofa on the opposite wall and a few side tables covered in candles. The whole place had a fairytale-like feel. It was appropriate. After all, we weren't considered real.

Through the open door was our little kitchen. There was an old-fashioned stove, an icebox, a crate filled with vegetables, and a basket filled with fruit. Within our cupboards were canned foods of all types, jams, jellies, and juices. Sitting atop the counter were two fresh loaves of bread — my favorite type, with raisins and sugar — and a bowl of boiled potatoes, carrots, and onions. I could hear humming coming from the bedrooms upstairs.

Sampson and Everest were standing behind me with gentle smiles on their faces. I bit my lip. How were they so gorgeous? It seemed impossible that I had randomly stumbled upon two beautiful men in the middle of the woods. Granted, we were one of the biggest and most well-known covens left. But still, why had they chosen to come to us? Perhaps they want to marry, I thought in the corner of my mind. Possibilities were swimming within me as I contemplated their motives.

"Hey, Marilyn! Can you come down for a moment?" I shouted.

I heard gentle footsteps pat down the stairs as Marilyn emerged in a gray dress that brought out the color of her light eyes. Her blonde hair was pulled into a braid, which fell down to her waist from the base of her neck. I smiled at her before gesturing toward the two men standing in our kitchen.

Her jaw dropped. "Who are you?"

"Everest and Sampson Silverstone, ma'am," Everest replied.

She blushed as he inclined his head slightly toward her. Marilyn was beautiful, and everyone knew it. Her little form and tiny waist were just two of the features that highlighted her natural elegance. I often felt like an elephant in her presence. Of course, I knew I wasn't larger than average. She was just so tiny that I felt huge.

"They came to find the coven," I said in a slightly-too-excited voice.

Marilyn's eyes grew wide. "Wonderful! I already made dinner. Let me just get some plates, and we can eat."

"Thank you," Sampson replied. "We're definitely hungry."

Marilyn blushed again before pulling plates out of the cabinets. I took a knife out and began to cut the bread. As the boys started to take their coats off, Marilyn shot me a look I could only interpret as pure excitement.

"Where did you find them?" Marilyn whispered.

"While I was out looking for the ingredients for the pain potion, they ran right into me," I replied.

"They're gorgeous!" she exclaimed.

"Trust me, I know," I mumbled back.

She flicked her hand, mumbling a quick transportation spell, and levitated the plates to the table. I followed her lead with our lemonade and bread. She gave me a little grin before sitting down at the table.

I walked over to the boys, who had settled in the living room, and smiled. With their jackets off, I could see their well-defined muscles and sharp collarbones. My stomach grew tight with the thought of brushing my hands against either of theirs. Sampson winked at me, which caused my face to turn a terrible red. I bit my lip before smiling back.

My eyes were still locked with his. "We're ready."

Sampson brushed past me, his fingers touching my waist. "Thanks, princess."

I thought I might melt right then and there. Every inch of my body seemed alive with sensation. He was grinning at me the way a fox might when smiling at a rabbit. My throat grew tight as I tried to contain the gasping breaths that were about to escape my chest.

Everest followed behind him and nodded. "Thank you."

"No problem," I whispered.

We had a tense meal where the hormonal energy was soaring. Everest was talking animatedly with Marilyn about their childhood. Their mother had been a witch, but they had never known their father. Their mother had refused to speak of him. He had clearly been a warlock, but they knew nothing more than that.

I listened carefully while trying to maintain a steady heartbeat. Sampson's legs kept brushing mine beneath the table. Each time we touched, he sent me a look that said he knew exactly how I was feeling.

After everyone had eaten plenty and was starting to get tired, Sampson and I volunteered to wash the plates. His body was so close to mine as I ran water over the wooden dishes that I could feel the heat from his skin. Each time I handed him a plate to dry, his fingers brushed mine. The touch of his skin was boiling and freezing at the same time. He caused my stomach to grow warm and my chest to shiver. As he finished drying the last dish, I began to step away. His closeness was driving me crazy. I couldn't think right. It was as if his very presence sent my hormones to the moon.

He grabbed my wrist, and I froze. My cells seemed to vibrate with a new intensity. How was he doing this? I knew practically nothing about this man. His name was Sampson, and he was a warlock but nothing else. Yet there was something within me, almost intrinsic, that made me want to melt in his arms.

"You feel it, too?" Sampson asked.

I met his blue eyes with a shaky tone. "Yes."

"I've never felt like this," he mumbled.

"Me either," I replied.

His thumb slowly moved to touch my jaw. For some reason, I nuzzled my face against his palm. I hadn't really intended to move toward him, but it had happened. My body no longer felt as if it belonged to me.

We both stopped breathing for a moment as he leaned down toward me. His hands traveled through my hair and down to my hips. He stopped at my little love handles and took a step closer to me. I could feel the heat of his skin and the sensation of his magic flowing from him like waves in the ocean.

My heart was beating at a speed I hadn't known possible. It was as if I had fallen from a cliff and soared through the sky. Everything seemed more intense. The oxygen in my lungs felt almost heavy. These sensations were different from anything I had ever experienced, and I certainly hadn't expected them. I had read about love in the old books on the shelves. Their torn pages and cracked spines revealed notions of romance from writers like Austen and Alcott. Even after examining the words within their mysterious depths, I had never realized just how the inside-out sensations of attraction could make you feel.

Until that moment, I hadn't thought much about falling in love. My dreams had been more of adventure and thrill than romance. Maybe it was because I had grown up in a world of single mothers, or perhaps I had just never known how euphoric it could feel. These tingling emotions weren't something you could accurately describe. No words were forceful enough to convey their intensity. My mother and aunt had made Marilyn and I study Shakespeare. Never before had I found it as interesting as I did when my face was inches from Sampson's.

"I don't know how you do this to me," he whispered.

"Trust me," I replied, "I have no idea."

Only a second later, his lips crashed down on mine. I jumped a little at first from shock but quickly recovered. This was the first kiss I had ever had, and it was wonderful. He seemed intent on smothering me to death, and I was very happy about it.

"You must be an angel," he mumbled into my hair.

I could taste his breath, hot on my cheek. Peppermint overwhelmed my senses. I bit my lip in response to the cool, clean scent.

"Thanks," I whispered back.

Before I had a chance to say anything else, he lifted me up and placed me on the counter. I gave a little yelp of surprise before sighing as he moved to place kisses on my cheeks.

When I closed my eyes, I could see bright colors flashing before me in an array of lights. His fingers were tight against my waist. No one had ever touched me with such skillful intent before. It was as if he understood my body and exactly how his hands made me feel.

I didn't even notice when another person entered the room. Everest cleared his throat when he saw us. My face flushed a bright red. I had been pulled out of my blissful unawareness and dropped into a puddle of awkwardness. Not knowing what to do, I averted my eyes. I heard Sampson sigh in annoyance as he turned away from me.

He looked over at Everest. "Hey there, brother."

CHAPTER THREE
ESME
REMEMBER

I knew I was dreaming as soon as I felt the heat of another warm body in the bed beside mine. Opening my eyes, I realized that my dream had taken me to another time and world. I was lying in a four-poster bed surrounded by a thick curtain that shielded me from the outside world. There were pillows all around me and blankets draped over my body. Gold, burgundy, and brown were all over the marvelous room. It was the type of scenery I imagined belonging in a fairytale book. I reached up to touch my hair. It was far longer than in real life. This dream world was manipulating everything.

I was wrapped in a long dressing gown made of rose-colored silk. It clung tightly to my body as I lay tangled in the blankets. The fabric was soft against my skin. It almost felt like cool ocean waves brushing against my waist. I could smell vanilla and cinnamon, but the scent was so far away I didn't care. The whole background of the alluring scene was intrinsically romantic.

The only thing I was completely aware of was the heat of a man's body beside mine. His arm was under my neck while my hand rested on his chest. I had never had a dream like this before. It felt so real. He was still sleeping. I could tell from his steady breaths that he was very content, and from the indications my body was giving, I was too.

It was just a dream, but endless questions still flooded my mind. Who was he? Why was I with him? And the more pressing question, who was I? As I examined the hard lines of his chest, I noticed a glimmering ring on my finger. It was plain, gold, and accented by a tiny ruby. I watched as it shimmered in the low candlelight.

I heard him take a deep breath and realized he was waking up. He shifted his body to lock down at me. I froze. The man was Sampson—older, taller, and with a slightly bigger brow, but still Sampson. How was this possible? Why was he in my dream? I didn't have enough time to process all the confusion overwhelming my mind.

Sure, we had kissed in the kitchen before bed. Nothing more had happened, though. This was a dream. It wasn't real. But why did it feel so true? His magic felt the same. There was no doubt about who he was. The feel of his masculine energy was flowing from his body to mine.

"Good morning, love," he whispered.

As he pulled me against him, he planted kisses on my

neck—the same gentle caresses I had felt before bed. He was so…familiar. His strong hands pushed at my lower back as he nuzzled me against his chest. I leaned into his touch. It was only a dream, but the scent of his body was so real. I could barely process the thoughts running through my mind, but something within me was sure I was enjoying the feel of his body.

He moved his lips to mine as I tangled my hands in his hair. His hands were silky yet firm, forceful yet soft. I wanted to melt into his arms and mold into him. He made me feel more beautiful than I imagined possible. I wanted him more than I knew I could ever want a man. The desire was overwhelming. And the strangest part of all—it was only a dream.

He smelled like ale, but not in a repulsive way. He wasn't drunk, just relaxed. His breath was fresh, though, almost like mint. Every aspect of his body felt familiar. Each thing he did heightened my desire. Why did I feel this need so intensely? He was almost like a shiny object I was being drawn to. His very touch made me want to let him consume who I was. Sampson—or whoever he was in this dream—was more than I'd known a person could be. He was almost too much.

"I love you, princess," he whispered.

My gasping breath was enough of a reply. I hardly had any chance to breathe between his kisses. Yet when he stopped planting them on my lips, he stole my breath with phrases I had never imagined I would hear.

The dream shifted, and I landed in a living room. It was the same time period as before — definitely in the colonial era, but I wasn't sure of the year. Along the walls were woven tapestries of scenes that must have been ancient. They portrayed women in their beautiful, natural glory. The first was a witch with the body of a tree and hair like leaves. Flowing from her hands was a river made of gold. It looked like the beginning of a story told to children. Perhaps it was a tale of joy or love. The next tapestry showed a man and woman in a tight embrace. Their hands were joined by a ribbon that wrapped their bodies in a swirl of moonlight. I could almost feel their happiness spreading through the room. Love like that could be felt within the souls of everyone who glimpsed it.

Little statues of animals, trees, and crystals lined the shelves. Candles burned in the darkness as a fire blazed at the far end of the room. Everest and Sampson, both dressed in brown, heavy clothing, were smoking cigars in tall, padded chairs. They looked just as handsome as they did in real life but different. There was something about them in this dream that seemed hardened and gruff. Everest's eyes still held their normal softness, though. They smiled at me after noticing my presence.

Looking down at my dress, I noticed the heavy cotton

fabric of a green gown. It had a full skirt, long sleeves, and a creamy undershirt. The fabric was gentle against my skin. It was heavy around me and did a good job concealing everything other than my upper chest. The boys didn't seem to mind, though. Their eyes still held the same heat.

Potted plants hung from the ceiling while flowers spilled over the sides of the tables. Soft light was pouring through the windows around the cream-colored curtains.

The smell of cookies spread throughout the house. Fresh bread lay upon one of the tables, a jar of marmalade beside it.

"Hello, Cassie. Come sit with us?" Everest asked.

And after that, I was sucked away.

CHAPTER FOUR
ESME
BACK TO THE GOODBYE

I awoke with a clear memory of the dream I'd had. My stomach felt as if it had been turned upside down. What did it mean? It was possible that it was simply a dream, but it could be more. I remembered Sampson's lips on mine, Everest's smile, and the warm heat of the fire. It was an odd dream. Every single part of it had felt real. Honestly, I felt there was a low possibility that my brain had randomly decided to place us in the colonial period. It seemed too strange to be a coincidence.

I slid from my cushioned bed to the floor below, where I threw a sweater over my little nightgown. The cool, airy fabric didn't do very much to protect me from the cold. I shivered in the chill air. The fire in my room had died. With a flick of my wrist and a small, whispered incantation, flames burst to life above the coals. With a swoosh of my hand, the candles began to blaze, too. I was no longer cold, just a bit chilly. Of course, the overwhelming sense of suspicion within my stomach couldn't be dulled by the fire.

I didn't have to move the purple curtains to tell that it was still dark outside. My bare feet tread lightly on the wooden floor as I opened the heavy French doors to step into the hallway. It was silent as I hurried to Marilyn's room. As soon as I reached her door, I walked in and closed it behind me.

She was buried beneath a pile of blankets. The only thing I could see was her blonde hair, as she was cocooned within the nest of cotton. Her bedroom was decorated with pastel shades of blue and a deep, heavy green. There were bookshelves lining the walls and carpets upon the floor. A large wooden light fixture with unlit candles hung from the ceiling. She looked like a child in the large bed.

When I reached her side, I gently shook her awake. Her eyes opened wide as she yawned. I felt a small sense of guilt for waking her but realized she would want to know about my strange, weirdly-realistic dream. Marilyn was always ready for a juicy bit of information to fantasize about.

"I need to talk to you," I whispered.

"About that hot make-out session with Sampson?" Marilyn asked in a still-half-asleep voice.

I blushed. "How did you know about that?"

She smirked. "The expression on your face when you came upstairs. Besides, I could pretty much see his energy flowing off you."

During any type of physical encounter, the energy between two people tended to mingle. When people engaged in such…heated encounters as Sampson and I had, the energy seemed to become one big blob that was almost impossible to pull apart. After a while, his energy would fade away from me. But for the moment, I was practically covered in his mystical essence.

"That's not why I woke you," I whispered.

She sat up. "What is it, then?"

I took a deep breath. "I had a dream. It was strange. Sampson was there, and I was—I was married to him."

She grinned. "Maybe it's a premonition."

I shook my head. "As amazing as that sounds, no. It wasn't in the future. It was in the past. From what I could tell, it was a pretty long time ago. It looked like the colonial period."

She raised her eyebrows while chewing on her lower lip. "Well, that's strange."

I sighed. "It felt real, Mari. It didn't even seem like a dream. I know it was, of course. But the emotions it caused weren't fake. I could feel everything in my soul. It sounds silly, but that's what it was really like."

She pursed her lips. "What else?"

"Everest was there, too," I replied.

Marilyn leaned back. "This is weird. It's too strange to only be a dream."

I shrugged. "I don't know what it is."

"We need to ask the Wise Women," she said.

The wise women were something like midwives combined with healers, leaders, and matchmakers. They were good at giving advice and very talented. I had always pictured them as the coven's grandmas. Most covens had several of them; ours had three. They were sisters and at least in their eighties. I had never asked them for help before, but this seemed like a unique circumstance.

I raised my eyebrows. "In the middle of the night?"

She stepped out of bed and began dressing. When she finished pulling her clothes on and smoothed her blonde hair back, she motioned to the door.

"You should probably get dressed," she said.

I nodded. "I'll go change."

When I stepped out of her room and into the hallway, I ran right into Sampson. I was in so much shock that I barely registered what was happening. He was wearing only thin, lightweight pants. Other than that, his body was displayed as a muscular maze that I wanted to dive right into. I brought my eyes up to meet his blue ones. They were clouded with something I couldn't exactly understand. His energy was tense. It was as if there was a vibrating force between us. I could practically feel the string connecting our souls.

"I had the weirdest dream," he said.

I tried to keep my eyes on his face, but they kept

traveling down to his hard chest and muscled abdomen. It took me a few seconds to process his words. Even as I spoke, my statement was a bit shaky.

"I did, too," I replied.

He tilted my chin up toward his face. Sampson's expression was a combination of anxiety and want. I had never seen anyone look at me with such need. It was as if I would disappear into a new world if I kept staring into his sparkling eyes. His full lips parted in a nervous smile. Only when his eyes started traveling down my body did I remember I was only wearing a little nightgown that fell to my mid-thigh and a fuzzy sweater. My legs suddenly felt very exposed as his eyes wandered over my long calves. How could something so little be so mesmerizing?

"We were married?" Sampson asked softly.

I could barely pull my eyes away from his chest, moving up and down. I bit my lip and managed to look back up at his eyes. He moved his own gaze back toward my face.

I nodded with nervous eyes. "Yes."

Neither of us had noticed that Everest was now standing in the hallway as well. When his eyes caught mine, I blushed so hard that my cheeks must have become strawberry-red. They matched my hair. Everest didn't seem bothered by it, though. In fact, he didn't even look fazed. He was perfectly calm and level-headed.

"I had a dream, too. I don't think it was exactly the

same as yours, but probably related," Everest said.

My eyes traveled between the two boys as we all held looks of awkward intensity and interest on our faces. There was only anxiety because of what this might mean. It wasn't a coincidence. These dreams meant something. If not for my curiosity — which I wanted to quelch — I would have tried to ignore them altogether. But I was too much of a theorist to forget the dreams. They would occupy my mind until I knew the truth.

Marilyn was now standing in our little huddle, too. "We should get going. I've already sent mystic messages to the Wise Women."

Mystic messages, letters transported through fireplaces, were our quickest forms of communication. They were like landline phones. The parchment covered in messy ink was cooler, though. We didn't bother with much modern technology — it wasn't needed.

Sampson's eyes were locked on my body. "I'll go get a shirt."

It took me a few moments before I could come up with a reply. His eyes caused a heated sensation upon my skin that I had to ignore. I felt like the sun was pouring down on me when his eyes were on my body.

I swallowed. "I should probably put something else on."

Everest, who had already changed into other clothes,

nodded in my direction. It only took a moment for him to avert his gaze. I wondered what his dream was about. He said it had been related but didn't give specifics. What was that supposed to mean? Was he hesitant to tell me? It gave me a nervous feeling in the pit of my stomach.

I put on a pair of soft pants and a sweater before stepping into my boots. I wrapped a cardigan around me, too. For some reason, I was freezing. I couldn't tell if it was the night air or the fear inside me. The anxiety shouldn't have been this terrible, but it was. There seemed to be a part of myself that knew what happened with the Wise Women would change my life forever. Because after we knew what these dreams meant, there was no going back. Somehow, my life had become tied to two men I had met less than a day ago. I wasn't sure how we were intertwined, but there was no questioning the connection; it was too clear to miss.

We made our way to the communal building in the middle of the village, where the Wise Women were waiting. A small fire burned in the center of the room. There was a pot, most likely for tea, boiling over it. The three women, each with gray hair braided or flowing down around their faces, gave us small smiles. They were like the advisors of the coven. Everyone respected them. The Wise Women gave me a sense of calm.

"Come sit, dear," the first woman said.

Marilyn made her way over to them. She sat before

lifting the teapot and pouring steaming cups for all of us. We watched each other anxiously. I was glad she was there because I would have been too scared to face this alone.

I sat between Sampson and Everest across from the Wise Women. Their eyes seemed to bore into us. Sampson's hand found its way to mine. I squeezed it tightly as our fingers laced together. Everest offered me a small smile that I returned. The silent words of comfort flowing between us were almost tangible.

"Please join hands," the women said in a unified voice.

I took a deep breath as Everest took my other hand within his own. Sampson simply brought the one he had been holding to his lips, where he lightly placed a kiss upon my knuckles. I couldn't manage to ignore the flutter in my stomach.

"Close your eyes and focus," the first woman added.

I tried to clear my mind as their chanting voices flooded my soul. It was an old unification spell. I had only ever heard it a few times before. It would be able to find the source of our dreams, as well as let the Wise Women decipher them.

Their voices began to fade away as my mind drifted back into another time. I immediately recognized the location. I was at the same house as my dream, but this time I was watching myself. It was as if I were a spirit in the room overlooking the scene. My heart pounded as I examined myself. I recognized that face upon my body. It wasn't exactly the same, but similar. There were more frown lines, heavier eyelashes, and plumper lips. My chest was larger, too.

It was a face I had seen every day. I didn't know how I had never realized the similarity before. Perhaps it was because the portrait in our living room was old and faded. Maybe I had just never looked at it long enough. Either way, I couldn't avoid reality anymore. The face I saw below was Cassandra's. Though I didn't want to acknowledge it, logic led me to the very obvious conclusion that was practically slapping me in the face. I was Cassandra.

I—Cassandra—was sitting in a chair with a needle and thread. It appeared as if I was sowing something. Then I noticed another surprisingly open fact; I was pregnant. Below the heavy layers of my dress and tightly bound corset, my pregnant belly jutted out. It wasn't obvious, but relatively clear if you looked at my stomach long enough.

I didn't want to watch this. I knew how this story ended. Cassandra, her husband, child, and former lover had died in a fire. It had been started by the people of a nearby village and had happened around twenty years after the Salem Witch Trials in 1713. They had all burned to death. Everyone knew about the tragedy.

Sampson, or rather Cassandra's husband, Constantine, entered the room. He placed a light kiss on my lips before pouring himself a glass of wine. He sat beside me and watched as my fingers laced the tiny pieces of fabric together.

I was making a baby dress. What a simple thing. This was a memory from my previous life. Of all the little moments for my mind to show me, this was the one it had chosen.

Everest, formerly Clovis, entered the room. He tossed what looked to be a peanut butter cookie to his brother before plopping down in a lounging chair. The room was relatively silent except for my humming. It was a lullaby, or at least it sounded like one. They all seemed entirely content. I hated that I knew this little family — my little family — went up in a mountain of smoke.

Everything went black as I was pulled away from the long-ago memory. I felt a little thud as I came back to consciousness. As my eyes were once again opened to the current scene before me, I let out a gentle, almost nonexistent sob.

Sampson

I was with Esme, but this time it was different. I was an observer of the scene. Her lips were crushing mine as we leaned against the strength of a cedar tree somewhere in a forest at sunset. Light danced around us as we were wrapped against each other. It should have been a painted scene. It was beautiful. Esme looked like a magical queen in her golden gown with ribbons laced through her hair. Her eyes were the most gorgeous shade of green I had ever seen. She was perfect in every way.

The grass was soft, with flowers scattered all around us. She was as entrancing as Sleeping Beauty. If she laid down for only a moment, I would surely fall in love with her. But her laugh was beautiful enough in itself. This girl was different from any other I had ever met. She was wild in a way that allowed her to be free, like a butterfly soaring through the sky. Her smile showed kindness and love.

My hands tangled in her hair as she placed kisses along my jaw. As I watched what seemed to be my former self wrap her in my arms, a realization hit me.

The girl I was holding was Esme. That much was clear. But she was also someone else I recognized. I had seen portraits of her, recreated sketches and even little statues. This girl, Esme, was Cassandra, the most powerful witch in history. The strong, fierce woman who had lived for love.

She had a huge smile on her face. "I love you, Constantine."

I watched as I kissed her back. My lips blended with hers as we fell into each other. Her thick dress was bunching up around us as I reached around to undo her corset.

I was Constantine: the warlock, warrior, and powerful husband of Cassandra. A tight feeling grew in my gut as I looked at the scene below. This was why I had felt an irrational passion for her from the moment I had first laid eyes on her body. Esme and I weren't strangers — we had been married.

"I love you, princess," I whispered as she laid her head on my shoulder.

A moment later, I was pulled away from my memory and thrown back into my seat beside Esme. As soon as my eyes opened, my eyes locked with hers.

Everest

I watched from above as this former version of myself talked with Sampson. We were in a dark room with a small fireplace blazing. It looked as if it belonged in a storybook. It was a scene I didn't want to watch.

"Look at this," I said.

I showed Sampson my arm, where a large cut was spreading infection through my triceps. It was a poisonous cut. I had heard of it before. Elderberry was fatal to warlocks and witches. The anti-magic properties caused the infected person, who could be exposed from a simple cut, to slowly fade away. It was like a wasting disease. But if a large amount was inserted into the body, it could kill the person quickly.

"Why didn't you tell me sooner?" Sampson asked.

"I don't want Cassie to know," I replied.

He shook his head. "You have to tell her."

I pulled my shirt down to cover the scratch. As I examined my former body, I noticed the darkness under my eyes and the shallowness around my face. The infection was spreading too fast.

"I'm going to try to find the cure," I said.

He stood. "I'm going with you—"

"No," I interrupted. "I want you to stay here with her. I'll make up some excuse about leaving, but I don't want her to watch me fade away."

Sampson was silent for a moment. His eyes carefully avoided mine. The tension in the room was practically screaming.

"I know how you feel about her," I whispered. "I'm all right with it because I know she feels something for you. Cassandra loves me, but she could learn to love you. And while I'm searching for the cure, a flower that may or may not exist, she might realize how she feels. If you learn to love each other before I return, I won't get in the way. She deserves happiness."

The scene became blurry as panic flooded my mind. Esme was Cassandra. It all made sense. I had felt drawn to her almost immediately, but I just thought it was chemistry. That was true, but it was also a connection from our former time together. We had been lovers. I was Clovis, my brother was Constantine, and Esme was Cassandra. Fate had brought us back together. The first time hadn't gone so well, and now it was time to try number two.

"I'll keep her safe," Sampson replied.

I drifted away from the scene as everything went dark.

When I opened my eyes, my hand was still in Esme's. My knuckles were white, and sweat was dripping down my forehead.

Esme

The Wise Women looked at me with serious expressions on their faces. Marilyn was looking between the three of us. She wanted us to say something. How could I tell her?

"What is it?" Marilyn asked.

The first Wise Woman's face met mine. "The vision was from 1713. She's Cassandra."

CHAPTER FIVE
ESME
MY FOREVER LOVE

I wasn't ready for this. It was too much. These flashbacks were causing chaos. My stomach was uneasy as I dashed away from everyone and made my way to my favorite place.

This little alcove was where I loved to be. It was a small place tucked away in the corner of the woods. I had started retreating here when I was little. When things seemed stressful, or I just wanted some quiet, I came to my little kingdom. I felt like I had some influence over what happened in this little corner of the woods.

The forest floor was made of gentle moss. A waterfall with smooth rocks below tumbled down to create a small pool of water. Trees overhead were linked by Spanish moss, which seemed to create a cloud above me. It was safe. I could relax when I was tucked away within the confines of my little fortress. This place seemed like a hidden location where I could vanish from the chaos.

I sat upon a smooth rock and pulled my cardigan tight around me. Tears began to trickle down my cheeks as I closed my eyes. I didn't want to think about any of this. Perhaps some girls would have loved this discovery. They might have enjoyed the power it gave them. But me, no. It felt like a true burden. I had to live up to Cassandra—I had to live up to who I was. Within a few hours, my life had changed. I could no longer be just a girl who happened to do magic. I couldn't be only a member of the Black Hills Coven. Because of this discovery, I had become so much more. I was Cassandra, the most powerful witch in history.

What was I supposed to do about Sampson and Everest? In my former life, I had been in love with both of them. Now I had a chance to redo all of it, yet I had chemistry with each of them. Yes, I had electricity with Sampson. It was like waves of tension that flowed between us at all times. When he took a breath, it was almost as if my lungs were also flooded with air. He felt like a part of me. Our souls were constantly dancing with each other. I could hardly control my urge to run into the safety of his arms. The coil in my stomach tightened when I looked at him.

But Everest, he gave me a warm sensation that flowed through my abdomen, too. His eyes caused a blush within my cheeks that made me look like a strawberry. I wanted to brush my hand against his every time I saw him. And when he looked at me, I felt as if I could spill my soul upon his hands.

He seemed to be a real knight, so noble and pure. Everest was the kind of man who would step in front of a sword to prevent it from grazing me. Though most of our communication had been through eye contact, I could feel the relief my soul felt at the sight of him.

"I'm sorry if I'm interrupting you. I didn't mean to infringe on your space," Sampson whispered.

He must have followed me. If not, he had used a tracking spell. That seemed like a lot of work just to witness my tears. Besides, he had his own problems to sort out. We were all dealing with a lot of emotions.

I tried to wipe the tears from my eyes. "It's fine."

He sat down on the rock beside me. His lips were pursed, and his eyes held a tired expression. I gently placed my fingers on his. Our eyes met with fire. I could feel the energy sizzling around us. He made me feel miniscule. I had never been small, but his tall form made me feel tiny. His shoulders were broad enough to easily encompass me in his arms, and his eyes seemed to show a compassion I wasn't sure I had ever seen in a man before. He was so hard but also kind. His personality was more complex than I could understand.

"I don't know what I'm supposed to say," he murmured in a gentle tone.

I laughed in exasperation. "I don't either."

His hand traveled to the side of my face. There was hesitancy. Last night we had kissed, but it was strange now.

Our new knowledge made everything feel different. Knowing you were sitting beside someone you had loved in a previous life was entirely odd. There was an overwhelming sense of familiarity but also a sense of awkwardness. Some part of me knew each inch of him, but another part of my brain told me to wait. It seemed crazy to rely on him for comfort — or at least that's what my so-called rational side told me. Yet despite all the tense energy surrounding our current state, he smiled. It was a real smile, the kind that felt like a precious gift. I could feel my resistance melting.

"I could fall for you. I think I already am," he said.

Butterflies seemed to be swarming within my stomach. I wanted to believe love could travel from one existence to the next. I hoped that some parts of ourselves could be transferred to new lives. And this moment, in its simple entirety, might show me the answer.

"I don't know what to do," I whispered.

He smiled. "I know. But while you're figuring it out, I want to fight for you."

Just the sound of his voice made my abdomen continue to churn and become tight. I felt all warm and tense. The anxiety caused by the smoothness of his tone was almost begging to be released. I couldn't keep waiting forever. Besides, he clearly wasn't bothered by my confusion. The uncertainty I felt seemed to affect me more than anyone else.

I chewed on my lip while he spoke. "I'd like that."

Before I had a chance to move toward him, he was against me. His hands pressed into my back as his lips fluttered over my neck. My eyes closed as I let my body blend into his. I felt like warm cookie dough being molded into a shape to match the curves in his body. He was the first man I had kissed, the first I had ever wanted to touch, and the first I had ever considered falling for. He was more sure than me, though. His kisses were like a battle cry. Sampson was positive of what he wanted. I was, too, sort of. He wanted me, and I felt the same pull toward him. The problem was, I wanted both of them.

Chapter Six
Esme
Pain and Sweet Smiles

I was dreaming again. It was an in-body experience. As I glanced around, I took in the lovely green grass, shining blue sky, and puffy white clouds. Birds were chirping in a nearby tree. Rays of sunlight illuminated my dark pink dress to make it look as if it were glowing.

My red curls were pulled into a braided updo that then tumbled down my back. A necklace of amethyst fell to my chest on a strip of leather. Though my skirts were heavy and weighed me down, my feet were bare and lay upon the ground.

Spread around me was a picnic blanket with bread, cheese, and wine. Berries and jam were also in the mix of food. I picked up a piece of cheese and began tasting it. The flavor of white cheddar immediately enveloped my sense of taste and smell.

"Cassandra!" Clovis — Everest — called.

I looked back at him with a smile on my face. I stood as he dashed toward me to wrap me in his arms and lift me into the air. He laughed as he began placing little kisses on my cheeks and lips. It must have been more of a memory than a fictional scene because I couldn't control how I reacted. I laughed before wrapping my arms around his neck and pulling him forward for a kiss that I initiated.

Without a moment's hesitation, he grabbed my hips and squeezed me tight against him. Emotion flooded me as his lips turned tender with love. It wasn't my thoughts, feelings, and needs. No, it was hers. This was all Cassandra. But since I had been Cassandra, who exactly did that make me?

Was I some cheap knockoff of the most powerful witch ever known? We had the same soul, so did that make us the same person? I clearly felt the repercussions of her past. Since the moment I first saw Sampson and Everest, I had known there was something special about them. We had all felt it.

But I had my own—Esme's—memories and feelings to connect with, along with all the complications resulting from my past life. So was I Cassandra with a few more stories to tell? Did I simply add this life onto the last one? Emotionally, it seemed like we had picked up right where we left off.

This dream was another memory to add to my list. My soul, which had ended up in two very different time periods, had so many details to recall. Seeing Sampson and Everest had certainly triggered the memories to come flooding out of some secret place within my mind. Now, it felt as if the two parts of myself were meshing to become a new person. I hoped I would like her. Because truly, she was me.

I was pulled back to focus when the dream shifted as Clovis moved away from me. My eyes locked with his before he cupped my face in his hand. We stood there for a moment before speaking. The silence wasn't bothersome but rather peaceful. My chest wasn't tight, but my abdomen felt as if it might turn my whole body into a melted pile of mush.

He reached into his pocket, revealing a tiny ring carved from quartz. It was a pretty pink that made me think of fairy dust and sunrise. I watched in fascination as he slowly slid it onto my ring finger.

Coming back to my own mind for a moment, I realized I had never been told this part of the story. I had known Cassandra and Clovis had been in love before she married Constantine, but I hadn't realized how far it had progressed.

"What's this for?" I asked.

He smiled. "I want everyone to know how much I adore you. I know you're only sixteen, and everyone says it won't last, but I don't care. I'll love you until I die, Cassandra. And whether or not I remember this life, I'll love you for as long as my soul exists. No matter when or where, I will always be hopelessly in love with you. You're all there is for me, baby. You are my epic love."

I could hardly breathe. But it wasn't just my dream self

that was frozen—it was me too. Clovis—Everest—had just been about as romantic as one could be. To speak of love in such a way, it really had to be magnificent. It wasn't fleeting or a phase. The type of love he had professed was the one that lasted forever. And apparently, it had.

"I don't know what I'm supposed to say," I whispered.

I felt everything Cassandra had felt in that moment, but more. I felt happiness, love, conflict, fear, need, and want. My throat was tight with unspoken promises. *If only we'd known*, I thought.

"Just say you love me—that's all I want to hear," he replied.

It was so strong. The desire and pure, untamed love she had felt in that moment was overwhelming. Cassandra had married Constantine. But Clovis, he had been her first love. Where did that put me?

I took a breath. "Yes, I love you. I love you so much."

He wrapped me in his arms again, his chest firm against mine. Even though I wasn't in control of my actions, I was all right with lying against him. How could I possibly not want the type of infatuation he described?

Still, my mind roamed back to Sampson. I wanted him so badly. He seemed to understand me on such a basic level. We practically mirrored each other when it came to connection. And when I thought about how he made me feel, I wanted to crumble.

I woke up with my forehead covered in sweat and my head burning with a headache. I must have fallen asleep after returning home without even bothering to change. Thinking about how Sampson and Everest were likely both asleep in a bedroom down the hall, I pulled my quilt back over my head and closed my eyes. I didn't have the energy to think about them, and I certainly didn't want another memory/dream to attack me in my sleep. The exhaustion was starting to take over. Confusing dreams like the one I just had left me tired. They certainly weren't restful. As I felt myself drifting off, I saw nothing hinting at the nearness of a dream. Maybe, if I tried hard enough, I could get a few hours of memory-free sleep.

CHAPTER SEVEN
EVEREST
FAREWELL, LOVE

As soon as I lay down, a dream consumed my thoughts. I was starting to get annoyed by these memories. Now that I knew they were instances from my past life, their presence bothered me even more. I was starting to think that nothing in my previous life had been remotely pleasant. After all, I had gotten sick and then practically handed my girl over to my brother in a wedding dress. And then, like an absolute idiot, I had moved in with them. Talk about a lousy past life experience. I was partly convinced I may have preferred not knowing.

The first time I saw Esme, I wanted her. But when I had noticed the desire in my brother's eyes, I knew the chances of making her fall for me were slim. He always got the girl. It probably had something to do with the stereotypical tall, dark, and handsome thing. Me, I was just the brooding, quiet brother resigned to letting him have the first pick. Not like it mattered what I did — the girls always chose him.

The dream took me to what appeared to be a bedroom. The sun was low in the sky, and candles were lit all around the room. I smelled vanilla and lavender. So feminine, so... Esme.

She was sitting on the bed in front of me. A ring, though not one from a wedding, was on her hand. Her heavy skirts were gone and had been replaced by a white nightgown that fell to the floor. Her curls flowed freely down around her as she smiled up at me. Though I was in my own body, I couldn't control my actions. It was a memory, not a fantasy. But when I reached down to touch her cheek, I imagined it was by choice. Because, oh, I wanted to touch her.

"I have something I need to tell you," I said.

My voice had come out deep and scratchy, almost as if I was trying to hold back tears. It didn't take me more than a few seconds to figure out what scene this was from. Why could I never glimpse happy memories? There had to be a couple.

"All right," she replied.

I took a deep breath. "I have to leave, love."

Her face turned dark. "For how long?"

This time, I could feel the tears behind my eyes. Whoever claimed that men didn't cry was wrong. At times like this, when I was giving up the one girl I would have done practically anything for, I had every right to cry. I was

walking away from her and couldn't even tell her the truth.
Sure, I could have explained the whole situation. But if I told
her how probable it was that I would die, she would be more
hurt than if I convinced her I had fallen out of love.

"If you want the truth, probably permanently," I
replied.

Her face had fallen as panic began to spread through her
gorgeous green eyes. I hated myself for what this was doing
to her. And honestly, as my present-day self, I understood the
faulted logic. There was no good way to deal with this. She
would have ended up hurt no matter what I said.

"What? You can't," she murmured.

I closed my eyes. "Look, I need to be alone."

She bit her lip. "You don't want me? What about our
supposedly epic love?" She pointed to the ring on her finger.
"This was supposed to be the symbol of our permanence."

The "supposedly" she had added in there stung.
It was epic. And even after three-hundred years, I felt the
long-lasting effects. Anger was bubbling within her and self-
loathing within me. I was going to wake up with a headache.

"Cassandra," I whispered. "I need you to be strong."

She looked practically furious. "I want you."

I hated watching this. It was a dream but also a memory.
And this memory made me want to punch something because
hurting her so horribly hurt me.

"I think it's healthier for us to be apart," I whispered.

She stood from the bed and approached me. "I know you love me."

I was trying to not fall apart. "I did love you."

She looked at me in shock. This dream was miserable. Why couldn't I have one of the nice ones? Sampson seemed to be enjoying his. Of course, they were probably the exact opposite of mine. He had ended up marrying my girlfriend. True, I had approved it. Honestly, that made it hurt even more. I must have been incredibly stupid. I wondered if my intelligence had improved.

Tears were tumbling down her cheeks. "You can't go."

"I have to," I whispered.

"Why?" Cassandra mumbled through angry sobs.

I could feel Clovis's stress — my stress. Looking at her hurt. Every bone in my body was aching with need for her. This memory was terrible. I wanted to know what it was like kissing her. I wanted to feel her tucked into my arms. Honestly, I wanted to be my brother.

"Love," I mumbled into her ear. "You need to be strong for me."

"I don't owe you anything," she said, pushing me away.

I needed this to happen. I needed her to be angry. But still, it hurt. I would rather her be furious than heartbroken. Her lips were parted in the gentle way I loved. I wanted to kiss her one last time. But if I did, I might not be able to pull away.

I nodded. "I'm so sorry."

She didn't reply as I started walking toward the door. Every step I took felt like a decade away from her. Before I left, I decided I needed to tell her the last part of my plan.

"Constantine is in love with you," I said with pain dripping from my tone.

Her breath caught, but she didn't give any verbal response. Maybe it was better that way. I didn't want to know if she had feelings for him. Because within a matter of months, they would be in full force. Not because she wasn't loyal but because he was so good at getting what he wanted.

The dream had consumed my mental state. Clovis's thoughts became mine as I blended into him. After all, we were the same person. It seemed that we were picking up right where we left off.

When I woke up with a sick feeling in my stomach, the first thing I thought of was her. Samson was in a bed only a few feet away from mine. He was asleep with a relaxed expression on his face. But Esme — Cassandra — was just a few feet down the hall.

CHAPTER EIGHT
ESME
OFF THE CLIFF

I walked quietly down the hallway in search of Marilyn. I could smell pancakes and cinnamon in the kitchen and began making my way down the stairs. When I woke up the second time, after a few hours of memory-free sleep, I knew I needed to talk to her. My feelings were a jumbled mess, and she was the only person I felt comfortable confiding in. She would at least attempt to help me work through my bizarre set of emotions.

When I stepped into the kitchen, I didn't see Marilyn. Instead, Sampson was standing beside the table with a bowl of strawberries in his hands. Already spread out on several plates were pancakes covered in syrup. A pitcher of orange juice was out, too. He had made breakfast.

Sampson smiled. "You're awake."

I nodded, not sure of what to say. There was so much tension—not in a bad way—between us. There were so many words, but I wasn't sure which one was right. I felt a thousand little things bubble up in me. Dé jà vu in its fullest form. What had his dreams been about?

Before I could give much of a reaction, Everest entered the room. It seemed for a moment that time stood still. All three of us were looking at each other. It was the first since our meeting with the Wise Women when we discovered our past identities that we were all together. I tried to shake it off but couldn't help but sense the triangle of tangible energy. There was so much power linked within the three of us.

Marilyn came skipping down the stairs humming a happy tune. When she reached the kitchen, some of the tension seemed to fade. Her expression became wide with shock.

"Have you all just been standing here staring at each other? Talk about awkward," she whispered.

A slight chuckle escaped from Sampson's lips. "Let's eat."

Marilyn grabbed my hand and pulled me toward the table. She plopped me down right beside Sampson and motioned for Everest to sit beside her. The room was silent again for a few moments.

Sampson's hand found mine under the table. "Pass the pancakes."

The sensation of his fingers against mine made my stomach twist. It felt good, but it also caused a small bit of guilt to flow up inside me. Everest's eyes were trained on mine. We were locked together by our gazes. Sampson didn't seem particularly aware of my interaction with Everest. His left hand moved to my thigh as he used his right to eat a bite of fruit.

"So...," Marilyn began, "am I going to have to be the leader of this supernatural therapy session?"

Sampson shrugged. "I'm perfectly fine."

Everest raised his eyebrows before using his knife to cut his pancakes. His body language was almost frustrated. He wasn't making eye contact with Sampson. I found the dynamic interesting. At first, I hadn't realized how different they were. Yet now that I was watching them in a tense situation, I saw their individual characteristics.

Everest was more quiet, tight, and reserved. Eye contact was a big part of how he communicated. He could speak silently through just a few glances. There was something distantly romantic about him. He wasn't confident or overpowering. Instead, he had a simplistic way of complimenting me through small smiles. He made me want to touch his dark blond hair. It was currently pulled back behind his head, but I felt a desire to release it from its hold. If his hair had been allowed to flow freely around his shoulders, he would have looked like a lion. His power was soft but not in any way fragile.

Sampson was the opposite. He was a bit arrogant, but in a way that I found intensely attractive. His dark hair and beard made him look like a mysterious man from a romantic fairytale. Touch seemed to be very important to him. He was good at it, too. His fingers frequently found their way to mine in a gesture that made the butterflies within me go crazy. And at the moment, with his hand on my thigh, I could barely focus on anything else.

The two brothers were night and day. And I felt so selfish because I wanted both of them. I wanted to be stuck halfway between the light and dark. There was a part of me that wanted each of them. It made me feel terrible. Why couldn't I settle for one? I knew the true answer. As Cassandra, I had loved both of them.

Marilyn was happily chatting away with Sampson, whose hand remained on my thigh, while Everest sat silently. I felt like an observer of the interaction rather than a participant. Eventually, everyone finished eating. I stood immediately to clear the table, and Everest followed along behind me. Sampson's eyes were trained on us as we began washing the plates. This odd, three-way relationship was going to become draining if we didn't address our underlying emotions.

Somehow, the tension in the room rose again. Everest was avoiding any form of contact, but his eyes continued grazing my body as he dried the dishes I handed him. We were brushing each other in more of a metaphysical sense.

When I felt a hand touch my waist, I knew it was Sampson. Everest's eyes had returned to the ground. Why was he so insecure? Was it because he had lost me last time? I didn't even know the reason as to why Cassandra and Clovis had ended their affair. No matter what, our former relationships didn't have to predict our current ones.

The air seemed to be dripping with testosterone. It was evidently making Marilyn uncomfortable. She pursed her lips and raised her hands as if to say, "I don't know what to do." "I think I'll step outside for a few moments," she said.

Sampson smiled at her before she sighed and headed out the door. He was the only one who seemed to be partially unaffected by the intense level of awkwardness.

Being sandwiched between them at the small kitchen counter was somewhat pleasant but more stressful. It seemed as if Everest was trying to blend into the wall, and Sampson was making an effort to touch me as much as possible. I liked having them both there, but the amount of sheer energy between the three of us was so strong it almost gave me a headache.

After the dishes were done, neither of them seemed to know what to do. We all stood there for a few moments without moving. At least the task had brought movement into the equation. Now we were just standing like three statues about to burst with emotion.

"Why don't we go sit down?" I said.

Sampson nodded. "Good idea."

Everest followed us into the little living room. The

seating arrangement only brought more tension. Sampson sat beside me on the couch and placed his arm over me. Everest sat in a chair a few feet away. I sat as still as possible. Was I supposed to talk first?

"Maybe we should talk about this," I whispered.

Everest glared at his brother. "You certainly didn't waste any time."

I almost jumped a little. It was the first time Everest had protested Sampson's apparent claim on me. His tone of voice was irritated and resentful. What had his dreams been about? I had never asked.

Sampson looked at him with a confused expression. "I made my move before we even knew about our past lives."

"Well, now that you know, you should at least give her a chance to think about it," Everest said in a clipped voice.

"I'm sitting right here," I whispered.

They both became silent at the sound of my voice. What was I supposed to say? I didn't know what I wanted. I couldn't decide in a few moments. It would have been irrational.

"What do you want, love?" Sampson asked.

"For you to stop fighting," I replied.

Guilt immediately crossed both their faces. They evidently hadn't realized how much it had been bothering me. Well, they were going to learn. I didn't want to cause a divide, but it was about three hundred years too late for that.

Before anyone had the chance to reply, a scream from

outside caused us all to jump in our seats. It was Marilyn. I knew her voice, and I knew she rarely ever screamed.

I dashed out the door with both boys following me. But as soon as I landed on the walkway, I was met with the sight of an envelope addressed to me. The paper looked old, almost antique. I ripped it open, not sure what to make of it.

Esmeralda,

It's a pleasure to finally communicate with you. I've been waiting for a while — about 300 years, to be specific. There's no easy way to explain our complicated situation, but I will explain the specifics when you arrive to retrieve your friend. She will be unharmed as long as you follow all of my directions. Please use the map within the envelope to help you find your way to my residence.

I look forward to seeing you tonight,
Gregory Silverstone

PS: I'm anxious to meet my sons. It's my understanding that you've recently become acquainted. Don't worry. All will be explained soon.

I froze. Marilyn had been kidnapped. But I wasn't particularly shocked with the kind of luck we'd had within the last twenty-four hours. It fit right in with the craziness.

What was the last part supposed to mean? He was Sampson and Everest's father? They had never known their dad. None of this made any sense. Still, we didn't have much of a choice in the matter. We had to go meet the man, or he would hurt Marilyn. I wouldn't let that happen.

I turned around to look at both of them and held the letter out. Sampson was the first to take it, so I let him. He scanned over it for a few seconds before placing it in Everest's hand. After a few moments, they were both looking at me.

"Well, I guess it's time to go meet Dad. This is probably the worst invitation to a family reunion I've ever seen," Sampson said.

Everest was deep in thought. "I don't particularly want to meet the man. Still, we have no choice."

I sighed. "Let's pack our bags. Looks like we're going on a trip."

CHAPTER NINE
ESME
WHEN WE FALL

We followed the map through the woods to what looked to be an abandoned castle. At one time, it had most likely been a pretty estate. Vines and thorns now coated the walls as they grew up and around the stone monstrosity. It looked a bit like the castle from Beauty and The Beast.

The trip had been uneventful—we had all been so focused on helping Marilyn. As we worked together, our focus had been solely on the mission. We worked well as a team when everyone was cooperating. If the tension was low, we could accomplish a lot.

My black pants were dirty with mud, and my hair was drenched with sweat. The boys looked considerably better. Apart from a bit of perspiration, they looked all right. I sighed. I was going to have to take on this crazy kidnapper looking like I had just emerged from a swamp. Huge confidence booster.

"Where do you think we should try to get in?" Sampson asked.

"We could try the front door," Everest said in a dry, boring tone.

Sampson cocked an eyebrow. "Fine with me."

I followed them as they made their way to the giant doors. At first, it seemed we couldn't open them. When pulling and pushing didn't seem to work, I waved my hand, muttered a quick opening spell, and watched as the doors creaked apart.

Everest pulled the door open wide and motioned for Sampson and I to enter. We both stepped in quietly, not sure what we were entering into. The room was dark, and I could barely see. It was cold and damp, making my throat feel dry and achy.

Sampson grumbled something about living in a haunted castle before snapping his fingers. Instantly, a ball of light began to illuminate the space around us. When I looked up, I was in awe.

The furniture was ancient—not replicated antiques, but truly old wooden structures. Cobwebs were everywhere, and the room looked as if it hadn't been touched in years. The large fireplace was empty. The room must have once been gorgeous yet had simply fallen into disrepair. It only took a little imagination to imagine what it could have been. The image itself made me admire the space.

Large carpets covered the floors while tapestries fell from the walls. The furniture was covered in dust, and the tables were coated in a layer of dirt. The floor was creaky, and the windows dark. Empty lanterns hung from the walls while candles decorated the space. They were unlit and old, almost as if they had been frozen for years. I wanted to imagine why a space like this went unused. If taken care of, it could have been stunning—fit for royalty. But in its current state, you would probably have to pay someone to live there. Of course, a few spells could do a lot to clean it up. If the man was a warlock, why didn't he use magic to fix the place? Perhaps he didn't want it. If he was here alone, he might have felt no need to keep it up.

Sampson and Everest seemed unimpressed by the large room. They examined the space as if it were a crime scene. Their investigative attitude would have been funny if my best friend wasn't the victim in the case. My focus was on Marilyn. Even as I walked through the beautifully distressed castle, my mind was consumed with finding her.

"Let's head upstairs," Sampson said.

Everest and I followed his lead as he traveled up the staircase. It was beautiful, the type one might find in a picture book. For a moment, I imagined walking down it in a ballgown. Walking down to whom? I didn't know. Ideally, it would be both of them, but that was selfish. It was improbable, too. I couldn't keep them both. It would have driven us all over the edge. The tension would be too high.

When we reached the top, torches lit the hallway. The floor, which was slightly tilted, was covered in a musty, twisted rug. It almost looked as if no one lived there. If they did, they certainly didn't have many visitors.

We heard a hushed voice at the end of the hall. A glance was exchanged between the three of us before following the noise. Everest had a sword strapped to his back. Sampson was armed with a bow and a quiver of arrows. I had two daggers strapped to my belt. We probably wouldn't need them — magic was more effective. Even so, it was nice to have them there for security. They were charmed, too. The arrows automatically reappeared in Sampson's quiver, and Everest's sword would return to him if it fell out of his hand. My daggers were charmed to burn like fire when they collided with a body. If I had to stab someone, their wound would be covered in flames.

Sampson had given us each a potion to make our movements silent. It was quite useful when breaking into a building inhabited by a kidnapper. I had never used it before, but it had been in one of my books. It was a helpful tool.

When we reached the door, I took a deep breath. Moments later, Everest gathered his bravery and opened the door. Sampson already had an arrow in his bow. My hands were on my belt, hovering over the sharp daggers. I had never so much as punched someone before. This would be interesting.

Light flooded my face as we stepped into the room. Lanterns were everywhere, and a fire was lit. The room wasn't dusty like the others. In fact, it looked nice, with plush sofas, bookshelves, and comfortable chairs. It was surprisingly warm. I wasn't sure what to make of it. This room felt comfy and alive, almost cozy.

Suddenly, a voice boomed from across the room. The tone was almost friendly, yet in a creepy way. I turned around to face him in a panicked frenzy. A chill went through my body. I felt sick but wasn't completely sure why.

He looked directly at me. "Ah, Cassandra. So nice to see you."

CHAPTER TEN
ESME
HELLO, AGAIN

"You don't get to call me that," I responded firmly.

He had called me Cassandra. Gregory — Marilyn's kidnapper — had called me Cassandra. I didn't want anyone to call me that, much less him. There wasn't much to say about him. He had gray hair and looked about fifty-years-old. For a man his age, he wasn't ugly, but I was still disgusted by him. Even if he had been the most beautiful man on earth, I would have been repulsed.

He laughed. "I apologize. Your name is Esme. That'll take some getting used to. You still look almost exactly like you used to."

So he knew what I used to look like? That wasn't a good sign. Was he another person from my past? If so, this kept getting more complicated. How could a former life affect me so much? This wasn't how I had expected my day to go. I wanted to have some blueberries and take a nap. Honestly, a little cake sounded pretty good too. Instead, I was stuck here with this maniac.

"Explain," I demanded.

He smiled in an overconfident way. "I knew you in your past life. When you were Cassandra, I was a member of your coven. I admired you, Esmerelda. You were, and predictably still are, a powerful witch. The most powerful ever known."

Why did these people keep popping up? Was I living in a world full of people from my past? Everything was hitting me all at once. Before yesterday, I had never known any of this. Now, it was starting to consume me. This was taking over every aspect of my existence. It was as if the world had simply been waiting to reveal my past. Now that it had been released, my life was a swirl of chaos. I just wanted to find Marilyn and take her home. I still needed to figure out what I was going to do about the boys.

"How are you still alive?" I asked.

He smiled at me for the second time. "I invented a potion to stop my aging. It's worked quite nicely. You see, things changed when I fell in love with a human woman. I told her I was a warlock, and you were furious with me. You said it put us all in danger. For my betrayal, you locked me in this castle. You ended up being right. She betrayed us. I've been here ever since. Every time I open a door, a magical barrier keeps me from stepping outside. With so much time on my hands, I was able to create the immortality potion."

Great, so he was the reason my coven had been slaughtered. He was the reason Sampson, Everest, my baby daughter, and I had died in our past lives. I was overwhelmed with anger. How could he even live with what he had done? I was right to have trapped him in this castle. He had put us in danger. Because of his stupidity, my daughter had died. I had never seen her in one of my dreams, but I knew she existed. It was part of the legend. I didn't even know her name.

"Well, as you can see, I don't remember anything you're talking about. So if you want revenge, you're a little late. I'm not the same as I was then. I've changed," I snapped.

It took so much effort for me not to lash out. I wanted to throw a dagger at him. He had practically killed us. And by some bizarre fluke of fate, he had ended up being Everest and Sampson's father in this lifetime. I wasn't sure I wanted to know how that had happened. It was entirely strange. Talk about a seriously complicated family dynamic. They hadn't even known who he was until this morning. Now, we all wanted him dead. First, we had to get Marilyn.

"Oh, no," he replied, "you misunderstand. I have nothing against you. I simply want you to let me out."

So he didn't hate me for locking him in a castle for three hundred years? Weird. I didn't have much of an urge to help him, but we had to go along with it. I needed my best friend back.

I raised my eyebrows. "Kidnapping my best friend probably wasn't the best way to convince me to help you."

"I had to get your attention. Besides, I wanted to meet my sons," he replied.

He was totally crazy. What kind of person used abduction as a way to attract attention? Only a total psychopath. He had some serious issues. I could hardly believe I was talking to such a mentally disturbed person. Spending three hundred years in this castle hadn't helped with his rationality, either.

Sampson and Everest were standing on either side of me, neither of them showing any emotion. They felt nothing for Gregory. To them, he wasn't their father. This was a man they were blood-related to, but nothing more. He wasn't supportive or loving, just a piece of this puzzle.

"I remember you two, too," Gregory added. "Your love triangle was intensely interesting. When I found out you were my sons, it was a surprise. Your past lives were the perfect picture of tragic romance. Cassandra — Esme — drove you crazy. From the look of things, she still has that same hold on you."

"If you've been locked in here, how are you our father?" Sampson asked.

We were all wondering the same thing. I wasn't sure I wanted to know the answer. He was definitely going to tell us, though. Gregory was a long-winded person. If we kept him talking long enough, it might be easier to figure out how to save Marilyn. Still, most of this information seemed tedious.

He smiled. "Your mother happened to discover my elaborate prison. She entered out of innocent interest and stayed for love. You were born in this building, son. When your mother discovered the truth about my identity, she fled with you and your unborn brother."

Disturbing was a kind word. What kind of old man lured a young girl into his prison to have a baby? She had probably had Stockholm syndrome. If not, she had been similarly troubled. Everest and Sampson certainly had interesting parents.

Growing tired of Gregory's crazy explanations, I asked, "Where's Marilyn?"

He looked at me. "She's safe. Don't worry. I wouldn't do anything to discourage you from helping me."

I could barely believe he actually thought his plan had been normal. Kidnapping? Really?! A simple note would have sufficed. I probably would have come out of sheer interest if he had told the truth. Granted, I may not have let him out. But still, kidnapping was never a good option. It wasn't even on my "top ten ways to persuade someone" list.

I rolled my eyes. "You mean, other than kidnapping my best friend?"

He gave a slightly psychotic smile. "I simply borrowed her."

Borrowed her? He was definitely a lunatic. Like seriously, completely insane. I hardly knew what to do. Sampson and Everest seemed similarly helpless. How were we supposed to reply? I had never dealt with this kind of situation before. Then again, most people hadn't.

I shook my head. "You're crazy."

Sampson touched my arm. "Let's get her and go."

Gregory made eye contact with me. "You won't be leaving without consequences if you don't free me."

Now he was threatening us. Not a good sign. He really did want out of this castle. At least I understood that. It was one of his only logical desires. The rest of his actions were just nuts. His motivations, though, I could at least process those.

"Show me Marilyn, and I'll think about it," I replied.

My head was pounding. Everything sounded crazy. But with what I had heard in the last forty-eight hours, it wasn't all that farfetched. This man was just another strange part of my new life that I could add to my list of crazy occurrences.

"Seems fair," he replied. "She's in the room down the hall."

CHAPTER ELEVEN
ESME
HEAL

I dashed down the hallway to the only other room with the door open. Sampson and Everest followed me. The room was lit by small candles, and the windows were boarded shut. It smelled musty and closed up. The scent was almost dungeon-like, hardly fit for human habitation. The windows probably hadn't been opened for hundreds of years. It looked more like a relic than an actual bedroom.

A giant bed stood in the middle of the room, with purple sheets and more pillows than I could count. The curtains on the windows were the same color. I wondered who this room had once belonged to. Whoever it was, they had probably been dead for a long time. Gregory probably hardly ever came in here. It seemed as if the only occupied room in the house was the one we had just left. It was a study of sorts and actually warm. He must have avoided the rest of the building. It really was a prison. This castle was the most elaborate cage I had ever seen. And the crazy part was, I was the one who had made it so. There were probably a lot of things about my past life I wasn't aware of.

Marilyn was tucked into the bed, barely awake. I ran toward her as my heart rate accelerated. Her head was covered in sweat, and her pretty blonde hair was plastered to her neck. Why did she look so terrible? It was as if she was sick. In fact, she looked truly ill. I focused on how hollow her eyes seemed. She was definitely miserable.

When our eyes met, she shouted, "Esme!"

I ran to wrap my arms around her neck. "Marilyn."

It was nice to feel her warmth. I could protect her. Guilt was spreading throughout my body. I was the one who had let her get taken. How had I been so stupid? This was my fault. Not only had I allowed this maniac to live, but I had enabled him to hurt Marilyn. I should have killed him when I'd had the chance. But if he had died three hundred years ago, I wouldn't have encountered Sampson and Everest in this lifetime.

"He gave me some kind of potion. Poison, I think," she replied.

Anger bubbled within my heart. He had no right to hurt her. Marilyn was one of the most innocent people I knew. She was so kind and loving. She was only sixteen. He had harmed her and infuriated me. Why had he said she was all right? He must have the cure. That's what he had meant when he mentioned consequences.

He was using the cure as leverage. I had to admit he was smart. This was how he would punish me. If I didn't let him go, she might die. But I didn't even know what spell would free him. I couldn't undo the prison magic when I didn't know how I had formed it in the first place. There seemed to be a lot of obstacles.

Still, I didn't want to let him out. He had done so much to hurt us. He was a madman. Who knew the terrible things he might do if I let him out? There were so many elements to this puzzle. How valuable was her life? She was simply too important. I wouldn't let her suffer because of his deranged ideas of negotiation.

"He must have the cure," Everest whispered.

"I know," I replied.

"I'm going to kill him," Sampson whispered.

I felt the same urge. It reminded me how truly alike Sampson and I were. We were both impulsive and protective. I sometimes let my anger get out of hand, and it seemed he did too. But in this case, we were right. There were two sides to this, and it was a very clear good and bad situation. There wasn't much gray.

Everest pursed his lips. "Probably not the best negotiating tactic."

He was right. Everest was logical. He thought ahead before doing something reckless. We needed his input. While

Sampson and I would have rushed ahead, Everest would create a plan. He might prevent a catastrophe.

"He doesn't deserve to be alive. Think of all the terrible things he's done!" Sampson replied.

Everest's face held annoyance. "If we kill him without getting the cure, Marilyn might die."

We needed the cure. I acknowledged that.

Sampson threw his hands up. "So we get it before we shove an arrow through his heart."

Everest sighed. "You're so diplomatic."

I watched them argue with interest. They were both slightly right. If we didn't get the cure, there was no guarantee she would live. I didn't know what he had given her, so I couldn't make my own potion to help cure her. It was a type of dark magic I had never worked with.

"I think we should kill him," Marilyn whispered in a light voice.

She looked so terrible, I wanted to kill him myself. Even though I could use my magic to do it, I wanted to use my hands. Some might say I was hungry for revenge, and that was fine. This was my best friend, and no one was allowed to hurt her without dealing with me.

"After we get the cure," I replied.

She smiled. "Don't worry about me."

I shook my head. "I'm not letting you become a martyr."

Everest reached down to take her hand. "We'll find the

cure."

For the first time, I noticed how similar Everest and Marilyn were. Selfless, considerate, and kind. These two beautiful blondes and they were gorgeous—were alike. I loved Marilyn. And Everest, I was starting to feel something for him. But it wasn't the time to think about it. Sampson was staring at me, and his mysterious blue eyes were practically devouring mine. I had met these brothers less than forty-eight hours ago—at least in this lifetime. But because of our prior bond, which seemed to be firmly rooted in our souls, there was already a seemingly impossible amount of devotion between us. I would have taken a sword to the heart for any of the three people in this room, but—excluding Marilyn—I wasn't sure why.

We needed to find the cure, and then I could kill Gregory. I wouldn't hesitate because it was my fault we were in this mess. My actions as Cassandra had led to this. Now I would have to deal with Gregory in this life, too. But it was okay because I had my favorite set of brothers with me.

CHAPTER TWELVE
ESME
WHEN THE SUN SETS AND FLOWERS FADE

"What did you do to her?" I hissed.

Gregory looked at me with an expression of boredom. "It was a simple enough poison. Don't worry. As I said, she'll be unharmed. I needed to find a way to keep her incapacitated. It would have been problematic if she had escaped. This was better than locking her in some desolate room downstairs. When she takes the healing potion, she'll be completely restored."

"You're a monster," I whispered.

"Call me whatever you want. I simply think of my tactics as successful," he replied.

Sampson and Everest were standing by my sides. We had left Marilyn in the other room so we could confront Gregory. It would be better if we took no chances with him. After all this time, he probably had a lot of ways to take us out. The danger surrounding us was enough to make me shake.

"You're going to hand it over," I whispered angrily.

There was fiery anger in my tone. I had never fought as hard as I was now — at least not in this lifetime. Total desperation had made me become a different person. It gave me a sense of strength I had never imagined I would feel.

He frowned. "As soon as you let me out."

I looked back at Sampson and Everest. They both had serious expressions on their faces. I wished one of them would talk. I didn't want to argue with him alone. Sampson looked as if he was trying to contain the murderous desire flowing through both our bodies, while Everest was afraid of what we would do. I was somewhere trapped in the middle. Maybe one of them was right, but I wasn't sure.

"I don't even know the spell," I replied.

He smiled. "I already thought of that. When you're ready, I'll hand it over."

I looked back at the boys. Everest was watching me while Sampson was watching their father. I could tell he was trying not to react. Sampson wanted to be irrational but was working not to. He was doing it for Marilyn and for me. A sense of connection fluttered within me. Sampson felt the devotion that I did, too.

"Give me the spell," I mumbled.

Everest sighed in relief, while Sampson seemed irritated. Not at me, but with the dilemma. This had no good ending, but Marilyn's life was more important than keeping him locked in here. Besides, we could just kill him as soon as we got the cure. He wouldn't get very far.

I had never felt the urge to truly harm someone before. It felt wrong but also right. I didn't really want to kill him, but I felt it was reasonable. This was a moral battle, but I knew which side would win. I didn't feel like myself. Cassandra was erupting within me. It made me feel authoritative. I was terrified but sure of myself.

Never before had I imagined my life would be so odd. Yes, I was a witch, but this was different. I was entirely adjusted to not being human. It was all I had ever known. I had grown up around witches, never realizing it wasn't average until I had grown older. But this was something I had never expected.

He smiled. "It's rather simple. Though no one in the world can do it except you. 'Key aperire'."

My heart was pounding in my chest. "Key aperire."

The air grew cold around us as a mystical wave seemed to flow through the room. I felt the openness. My soul swelled with the energy of my magic surrounding us in a flurry of freedom. He burst into a wide smile before pulling a vile from his pocket. It was filled with a silvery liquid that sparkled in the dark room.

"It's yours," he said, placing it in my hand.

I grasped the cure as if it was the only thing keeping me from falling into insanity. I felt the energy pulsing in it.

The potion was strong—it would heal her. I could feel the power. It was liberating.

"You're dead," Sampson whispered.

In less than a second, an arrow was notched on his bow and aimed straight at Gregory's heart. The older man seemed shocked. What had he expected to happen? Apparently, he thought that giving me the cure, which would stop an illness he had placed over Marilyn, would resolve our issues. That wasn't how these things worked. You couldn't kidnap and poison someone and expect to be friends with their family. I wasn't a big enough person to get over this disaster in a matter of moments.

I handed the cure to Everest and whispered, "Go."

He took the vile in his hand and dashed out of the room. I trusted him enough to put her life in his hands. That had to mean something. I didn't have time to think about it, though.

Sampson shot the arrow. It would have pierced Gregory's heart, but he reached out and halted it with his hand. My jaw dropped. This was going to be more difficult than we thought.

"Ah, son. I see you're still trying to be the hero to win the girl. Sadly, your brother will always have that title," he said.

Sampson's face darkened. "I'll find a way to kill you."

Gregory smiled. "You can try."

A chill spread over me. The room seemed to grow frigid. Something terrible was about to happen. I had a feeling, and it wasn't good. Miserable anticipation spread through me.

Sampson lunged for Gregory, but he moved out of the way. When Sampson grabbed his arm, they both tumbled backward onto the desk. I flinched as the objects went flying and papers soared into the air.

Everest and Marilyn dashed into the room. She looked completely recovered. At least Gregory had kept his word when he said she would be fine. They looked at me in shock. Everest immediately drew the sword from his back while Marilyn stood motionless. Neither of us knew what to do. We had never been in an actual fistfight, no less a real life-or-death altercation.

I grabbed one of the daggers from my belt and tossed it to her. Her eyes were wide with fear. Mine were, too, but this wasn't her fight. She wasn't part of this past-life revenge train. Still, what was I supposed to do? She was my best friend. I would have to drag her out to make her leave. I didn't have the energy for that. She was a witch, and I trusted she could use the dagger and magic to defend herself.

Sampson was attempting to take Gregory down again, but his repeated swings weren't doing much good. Gregory was too agile for his age. Granted, he shouldn't have been alive at all, but magic could do that sort of thing. We had no idea what he had come up with here. He had probably constructed potions we had no knowledge of. Though we had numbers, he had hidden skills and advantages.

Everest reached for Gregory but was pushed backward by a wind erupting from his hand. Gregory could make shields to protect himself from others. Still, he could only do so much at one time. I was going to have to join in on the chaos.

Everest was still fighting against the energy shield, but it wasn't working. He couldn't get within five feet of Sampson and Gregory. He was practically helpless. Every time he swung his sword, it bounced back. Sampson was still dedicating his attention to trying to hit Gregory. No matter how many times he attempted with his bow or fists, he was unsuccessful. Gregory was faster than I understood to be possible. Occasionally, he took an opportunity to swing back at Sampson. Most of the time, he hit him. Sampson's lips were split open, and his cheeks were splattered with blood.

Gregory didn't want to kill us. I didn't exactly understand why. Maybe it was because Everest and Sampson were his sons. Still, I didn't think that was the answer. He thought of them as Clovis and Constantine rather than their current identities. Most people seemed to have adopted that opinion.

I grabbed the dagger from my hip and swung. I had never been very skilled with weapons. Granted, this was a new type of situation. But even with regular knives, I had a tendency to hurt myself. I probably should have used magic against Gregory's talents, but I just didn't know what spells could hurt him. The dagger seemed a lot more sure.

I was able to pass through the barrier preventing Everest from nearing them. With my weapon ready, I lunged at Gregory. As I flung my hand forward, I closed my eyes. I didn't want to witness this. My target had been his chest, but I had no idea where the dagger would end up.

Sampson gasped, and I glanced up. The dagger was no longer in my hand. Gregory stood before me, perfectly fine. When I had gotten over the first bit of shock, I realized the room had gone disturbingly quiet. A small sob echoed through the space, and I turned to see Marilyn with the dagger protruding from her body. It had hit her heart.

Somehow, Gregory had transferred the dagger from my hand to Marilyn's body. I had never heard of that type of spell. It had to be intricate. I ran toward Marilyn as she collapsed onto me. My arms went around her waist as she fell to the ground. All I could see was her. Killing Gregory no longer mattered. These daggers were charmed. I had chosen to make them more powerful. The hole in her chest was on fire, and it was too late to stop it. No magic could save her. A wound to the chest was a hard thing to deal with. There were a lot of potions and spells I could do, but saving someone who was moments from the end wasn't something I could accomplish.

Tears were pouring down my cheeks, and sobs escaped

my body. My heart was fracturing. This was Marilyn, my best friend from birth—my twin flame. She was dying, and there was nothing I could do. It was as if the sun had vanished or all the flowers had disappeared. She was bright and beautiful. The colors seemed less vibrant.

Her pale skin was growing sickly. The brightness of her eyes was starting to dim. It was probably an illusion, but even her blonde hair seemed to look less alive. I could see the pain on her face. She seemed to be in too much agony to even scream. There was so much blood. Sixteen was too young to die. As she closed her eyes, I imagined she was in a peaceful sleep. Her soul left her earthly body, and I was left with nothing more than her lifeless form.

"Get out," Gregory whispered.

Everest moved to my side to pick her up. He lifted Marilyn into his arms and tucked her head against him. Sampson wrapped his arms around me and lifted me onto my feet. I could barely move.

"If you leave now, I won't harm the rest of you," Gregory said.

My body was on fire with anger. "No!"

Sampson wrapped his arms around me as I attempted to break away from his hold. I wanted to throw my dagger through Gregory's chest. I wanted him to feel what she had felt. Sampson's hold was too strong, and I couldn't break free. He wouldn't let me go.

"Sampson!" I shouted.

"No, Esme," he replied. "I won't let you go, not if it means he'll hurt you."

I wanted to be angry with Sampson, but I couldn't. He wanted to save me the way I had wanted to protect Marilyn. I couldn't fault Sampson for that.

My body was starting to feel light. My knees felt wobbly and frail. I was too distressed to know what to do. Sampson was there, though, holding me against him. Everest walked from the room with Marilyn's body in his arms. Without hesitation, Sampson wrapped his arm around me and began to follow them. I had one last look at Gregory's face, and it was shrouded in pacified satisfaction.

Chapter Thirteen
Esme
Whispers of Goodbye

Her hair was flowing down around her face. The pretty golden curls framed her cherry cheeks like sunshine around a flower. There was a desperate need within me to reach out and touch them one last time. Her lips were as red as an apple and set in a small smile. It was a peaceful sleep. In death, her pain was gone. Her blue eyes were concealed. They would always be covered by her soft, white lids and dark lashes. Never again would I meet the peaceful seas that were her eyes.

The wound in her chest was covered by a beautiful white gown that made her look like an angel. It was almost the same color as her skin. The lacy top fell around her body to create a pool of white cotton. She had wanted to wear it for her wedding, confident she would one day find a man to love. Even though most witches never made families with the human fathers of their daughters, she had been set on marrying.

Marilyn had always been kind, intelligent, and bright. Her personality had been fun and light. When she was around, my mood was lifted. She brought joy to every room. I needed her there to whisper with at night, to swim with in the summer, and create with when my magic felt too weak on its own. My best friend — my soul sister — was more beautiful than I had ever imagined being. In death, she looked like a princess.

Her hands lightly grasped a bouquet of daisies. She had loved them. It was only right that she was placed in peace with her favorite flower. Below her was a bed of dahlias. Their pink and purple colors brought out the ruby in her lips. She was a true princess, perhaps a Juliette. She was romantic, with dreams of love. And to me, she would always be alive. In sixteen years, she had made a bigger impact on me than almost anyone else. I wanted to hear her laugh again. Somehow, it seemed as if her voice would make things better.

I couldn't shake the feeling that it was my fault. If I, as Cassandra, hadn't imprisoned him in that mansion, he would have never hurt her. If we hadn't tried to kill him, she would be fine. Marilyn was a victim of the mess we had made. To the evil man that was Gregory, she was collateral damage. To me, she was a girl that had become a shining star. No matter how long she was gone, I would always see her in the beauty of the moon, stars, and sunsets. She would never cease to be my best friend that couldn't be replaced.

I hoped she would come back to me. I could barely imagine the next seventy years without her. Was she at peace? She had to be. Marilyn had been a true innocent. She had been naïve yet wise, impressionable yet strong. Hopefully, she would find the strength to forgive me. I would always love her and regret that her life ended before she had really had the chance to live.

Sampson and Everest stood behind me. They had helped prepare her for the funeral. I didn't know what to say, but people had come anyway. Our whole coven had gathered for the remembrance of a girl lost too young. Witches, young and old, placed flowers around her. Warlocks stood back with grim expressions on their faces. I saw the Wise Women in the back. Their faces held sadness, but their eyes were filled with hope. Everyone knew who I was. News traveled fast. I was Cassandra, and everyone was looking to me. They wanted my leadership, but I didn't know what to give them.

Sampson and Everest each offered me an arm. I took them both. Sampson was on my left, and Everest was on my right. They allowed me to lean on them. I wanted to curl up and cry, but I couldn't. I was Cassandra, and I could do this. Even if I felt weak, I had hidden strength to help me make it through.

I stepped up to her. Placing my hand on hers, I imagined I could feel her magic. It didn't work, though; her magic was as gone as her soul. They were somewhere else entirely. This body — her body — was an empty form. Still, I felt the need to pretend she could sense me.

Our mourning process was different from most humans. Acknowledging that her soul had already left her body, we returned it to the earth. Not in the typical burial fashion but through cremation. Our funeral pyres respected the bodies of the deceased but allowed us to give their ashes to the earth.

I looked down at the flowers surrounding her. "I love you, Mari," I said in a hushed whisper.

Sampson stepped up to take my hand and pull me away. I allowed him to wrap his arms around me while Everest stood at our side. They were both silent.

"Ignis," I whispered.

The fire burst to life in a flash of bright flames. The flowers went first. After I saw them turn to ash, I closed my eyes and turned away. People parted on either side of me as I walked away from her pyre, Sampson and Everest right behind me. We would come back for her ashes later. I simply couldn't watch. She wouldn't have minded.

I would spread her ashes in a field of flowers when it was over. For now, I needed to step away. Losing my best friend was hard, but knowing it was partially my fault made it worse.

Chapter Fourteen
Esme
Don't Go

My bedroom was lit by the soft moonlight and a few candles. Lavender filled the air, but the room seemed empty. There was a vase of flowers on my vanity and a bundle of roses on my bedside. They were the comfort people tried to give me. The kitchen was filled with baked goods. Mourning is a strange thing. No matter who you are, you do it. The sensation of numbing sadness is something universal.

I felt the frigid air and wind as it drifted through my window. My skin was dry and cool, but I didn't do anything about it. Some eucalyptus would have worked, yet I couldn't motivate myself to leave my bed. Blankets were draped over me as I sat staring at the wall. My hair was bunched up at the nape of my neck, and I wore a simple cotton nightgown. It was soft and warm, but it couldn't eliminate the chill within my heart.

Tears were dripping down my cheeks. I could have

wiped them away, but they were what I had left of her. They reminded me that she could never be truly forgotten. Even so, I looked like a disaster. I didn't really mind, though. Everything I felt was for her. Every inch of pain in my body had her name etched into it.

I felt like I had been stabbed. When I saw the dagger in her chest, it was like I was dying, too. The burn of rage had spread through my body like a screaming hurricane of fire. My throat had been dry and tight. It was like a ripple of pain had begun in my chest and spread through the rest of my body. The world had stopped, and I had been left with the overwhelming feeling that my life would never be the same. Darkness had descended upon me. Her loss had turned my mind into a jumble of anger, confusion, and pulsing pain.

I heard the door creak open. In the dark, I couldn't really tell who it was, but somehow, I knew it was Sampson. It was his energy and something else deep inside me that sensed when he was near. I felt as if a string went from my heart to his and wrapped us in a tight union that couldn't be broken. It scared me, but I didn't want to fight it. I didn't have the strength.

He wore a pair of heavy pants and a tight shirt. I could see the lines of his chest and the indents of his abdomen. His hands were stiff and squeezed into fists. Against my intentions, the coil in my stomach twisted until I could barely ignore it. I had to bite my lip to prevent a sigh from slipping out. His hair was lazy and wet — he must have showered. The scent of fresh mint was all over his skin. In the light, the water droplets made his face shine. I shivered from the closeness.

"I thought I should check on you," he said in a deep voice.

His very tone made my mind spin. I swallowed and tried to keep my body from freezing. This kind of reaction was almost unexplainable, or at least not average. I shouldn't have been so overwhelmed by a few glances. But I was because part of me knew. There was some bit of myself that understood us — understood him.

"I'll be all right," I whispered.

The warmth in my stomach was spreading. My chest was tight, and I could feel my breath catching. Everything was standing frozen. The wind was whispering lost words from long ago. It was wrong. I was mourning, and I shouldn't have wanted him. I did, though. It made me nauseous. Of all the emotions to be feeling, this was not the correct one.

"I wish I could believe that, love," he whispered.

His blue eyes were searching my mind. I could feel the heat of his gaze on me. There was a need and a softness to it. I wanted him to know the truth, but I was sure he already did. Sampson could feel the way my heart was beating as much as I could feel his.

"Me too," I replied.

He moved toward me and placed his hands on mine. I

bit my lip as our gazes locked again. I couldn't seem to escape him. Our bond was too strong. I reached up to place a hand against the side of his cheek. He closed his eyes and smiled. A shiver went up my side, and I saw his muscles tense.

"Will you let me take care of you?" Sampson asked.

I pulled him toward me and placed a light kiss on his lips. It was almost bubbly with warmth. There was a moment when I imagined things it might be better not to. I thought about my dreams—memories—that caused the flood of emotions to thunder through my chest.

"If you feel you need to," I replied.

His lips pressed against mine. We should have been thinking of Marilyn. But the way he made me feel, it helped cure the pain in my heart. It was a distraction, yet comforting. The bubbling feeling made the ache recede.

"I should let you sleep," he mumbled.

He was right. We should both be asleep. He made me feel, though. Right now, the numbing was too much. Touching him helped me. I didn't want him to go. Watching him leave the room was like allowing the tide to fade away. I would be cold again.

"Please stay," I whispered.

He took a breath. I watched the relief cross his face. Something changed at that moment. I wasn't sure what had happened, but when he opened his eyes, we knew the difference. There was a clicking sensation. A piece of the puzzle had finally arrived. We had changed — I had changed. I was becoming her. Cassandra and Constantine were pushing their way out. And after all their time apart, they were ready for a passionate reunion.

CHAPTER FIFTEEN
ESME
SISTER

Gregory had killed Marilyn, and I wasn't going to let it go. I wanted revenge. Maybe it made me a bad person or simply someone unable to forgive. I wasn't sure, but I didn't care all that much. Killing him wouldn't make me feel better, and it wouldn't make her come back, but it might give me a sense of justice. He had hurt me in this life and my last. He had caused the death of my family, and I wouldn't forget it.

Not only had he taken my best friend from me, but he was the reason I had died in 1713. At nineteen years old, my first life as Cassandra had ended. Gregory was the reason Sampson, Everest, and I had been burned alive when we had only begun to experience the world. My baby daughter had died because of his betrayal. I still wasn't sure how I felt about the knowledge of my past life, but I knew how it made me feel. My emotions and protective instincts were soaring. I had never felt so defensive. These people were my family, and I would keep them safe. And if I couldn't accomplish that, I would avenge them.

Sampson had held me as I drifted off to sleep. When I was in his arms, the nightmares stopped. I didn't dream at all. There were no memories or past life flashbacks. It was peaceful oblivion. Something about him calmed the raging sea within my soul like he had given me some sort of sleeping potion. I knew he hadn't, but his presence was enough to make me fall into a few hours of peace. The wheels stopped turning, and I was left to drift into a sky of blackness. Seventeen-thirteen didn't invade my mind when he was nearby.

When I had woken to watch the sunrise, Sampson hadn't moved at all. I was still laying on his lap with my head on his chest. I could tell he was awake, but his body was relaxed. Neither of us said anything. There weren't words to express how we felt. I just knew I needed to hold onto him the way I needed water. He kept me anchored, and I couldn't manage to untangle my fingers from his shirt. His hands were lightly placed on my hips as he laid a gentle kiss against my hair. The tips of his fingers traced little lines up and down my sides. I'd closed my eyes again and let the exhaustion take me.

Now I stood in the front yard as the wind blew against my face. My red curls flew in the breeze and traced a ruby trail behind my head. I was tightly wrapped in a blue sweater that protected my skin from the harsh weather. There was a frigid feeling in my cheeks and a chill on the top of my nose.

Marilyn's ashes were beside me, but I hadn't touched them yet. It would take a while before I was ready to return her to the earth. She had been my constant companion. We'd lived our lives side-by-side. I didn't want to let her go. It felt like losing part of who I was.

My skin still held the sparkling feeling where Sampson had held me. It was as if a warm, bubbly blanket of his energy was wrapped around my body. It was the only thing keeping me slightly sane. Just the reminder of his touch against my skin made me want to run to him.

I hadn't seen Everest since the funeral. He didn't seem to feel it was his place to enter my solitude. It was part of his personality, one of the things that defined him. Yet, in my selfishness, I wanted him near me. I wanted both of them. Sampson had stayed with me through the night, and now I wanted Everest to hold my hand as I made it through the day.

There was something wrong with me. I knew my life in 1713 was still affecting me — the way I had loved both of them and how I still felt a desire for them in my heart. My soul was linked with theirs, and each of us could feel it. Sampson and Everest consumed my affections, and I barely had a moment when I wasn't thinking of one of them. For a few seconds, I briefly wondered if it was possible to have two soul mates.

Everest

I woke up in the middle of the night to find Sampson absent from our bedroom. A nagging feeling had begun to creep through my body. Of course, I didn't want to intrude upon anything. Esme deserved her space. She was in so much pain that I didn't want to make this more complicated. I would wait for her to make her choice. No matter how long she waited, I would be patient. This was a hard period for her. All of us had been shocked by the truth about our identities, but she was also mourning. Her best friend had died. She wouldn't be the same for a while.

There was a need within me I had never felt for anyone else. I wanted Esme more than I could express. She was worth waiting for, even if it took a hundred years. I would wait for three more centuries if she would choose me again.

But I couldn't just sit and wonder where he had gone. We weren't safe right now. Gregory was out and roaming the world. He could be looking for revenge. We had attacked him, and he probably wasn't interested in letting it go. Clearly, his power was far stronger than Sampson and I had anticipated. We couldn't have a repeat of the same tragic result.

I stood from my bed and slipped on a shirt. My hair was a tousled mess, but I was barely concerned about it. The blond strands seemed to settle themselves with one quick brush of my fingers. Anxiety was coursing through me, but I tried to push it down. It wasn't right to invite myself into her room. I couldn't help myself, yet the guilt was pounding through my chest. I would just check to see if she was okay, and then I would go.

I made my way down the dark hallway toward her bedroom. For a moment, I contemplated turning around. I had no idea what I would see. She probably wanted privacy. My persistent curiosity and stress were too hard to ignore, so I continued down the hall. When I reached her door, it was already open.

I froze in anger and surprise. She was curled up against his chest. Esme was sleeping peacefully, and I resented Sampson for it. I wanted her to be happy, but I was furious that I wasn't the one bringing her rest. There was real, genuine anger in my heart. I had never felt so angry with Sampson.

Esme should have been mine to begin with. If I hadn't left her in 1713, there wouldn't even be a question about who she belonged with. I wanted her back, and I was determined to get her. Sampson was charming Esme, but I would win her. After all, she had originally fallen for me first.

It only took a few moments to notice that Sampson was awake. Our eyes met with a shared sense of defiance. There would be no brotherly affection when it came to her. I wouldn't compromise on Esme. This girl could be the thing that drove us apart. I didn't want to be angry with him, but there was something in my chest I couldn't get rid of. It was like a sharp pain that made me want to pull him away from her and throw him to the ground. I had never imagined feeling so passionately about a woman, but Esme was special.

With one final look at her peaceful smile, I turned and left the room. One day, she would love me. And when that time came, I would relish in it.

Esme

The cold wind was blowing around me when I saw a figure approaching from a distance. I could tell it was a woman, but not much else. As she continued to walk closer, I could see her white-blonde hair that looked as soft as cornsilk. Her platinum strands were straight as a ruler and light as white roses. She had pretty blue eyes the color of a sweet berry. They were the type painted in pictures of Renaissance women. Her lips were a soft pink, while her cheeks were rosy and chilled from the wind. She was regal.

A black cloak was wrapped around her body while a bow and quiver were strapped to her back. She looked like a warrior from ages past. I almost wondered if I was dreaming, but I knew she was real when she stopped only a few feet away from me. When my eyes grazed her face, I noticed how she reminded me of Lyssa, the Greek goddess of mad rage. She was powerful, overarching, and slightly scary. I wanted to imagine there was a softness within her, too.

I didn't realize the boys had come outside until Sampson's hand found mine. Everest stood protectively at my side. Compared to them and the mystery woman in front of us, I felt small. I was afraid of her, but not so much that I felt the urge to run. Besides, I had Sampson and Everest with me.

"Are you Cassandra?" she asked in a tight, tired voice.

I nodded. "Yes."

She relaxed her shoulders. "I'm Riona, and I'm here to help you kill Gregory Silverstone."

***

After taking Riona into the house, I made a pot of raspberry tea. The room was tense but not dangerous. I felt awkward, but not too much to be friendly. She was gorgeous, and I envied her clear, delicate skin. She was clearly a warrior, a woman versed in the art of combat, but she was still beautiful. Her blue eyes were almost as alluring as her pale hair. She looked as if she had been carved from ice and decorated with snow. Riona was the type of woman little girls thought of as a real-life princess.

I set the teapot on a small table in the sitting room before pouring several cups. After handing them out, I sat down between the boys, Riona, across from us. She had shed her outer cloak to reveal a tight leather vest that gripped her chest and fit like a corset around her abdomen. She wore a black shirt underneath and a pair of tall platform boots. Her pants were heavy cotton. She was outfitted for war. I didn't want to know where she had come from or why she had found us. I simply wanted to know how she planned to kill the man who had murdered my best friend.

Riona looked at Sampson before turning to Everest. "I should tell you everything. Boys, I'm your little sister."

Sampson cocked his head while Everest held a confused expression on his face. After the strange turn of events we'd had, it didn't surprise me. I could have been told aliens had arrived, and I wouldn't have been shocked. If a giant monster erupted from the earth, I would have sighed in annoyance. The death of my best friend had made everything feel bland.

Riona continued after a few moments of silence. "We have a different mother, but Gregory is my father. Unlike you, I grew up with him. I didn't know you existed until my mother discovered the secrets he'd been hiding. She found one of your mother's diaries. It was filled with the truth of who Gregory was and how your mother planned to protect you. When my mother read it, she knew we had to leave. Two years ago, my mother and I tried to escape. Gregory found out before we left and killed her. When I finally found a safe place to stay, I knew I had to find a way to avenge her."

"How old are you?" Everest asked.

"Sixteen," she answered.

Sampson leaned back and wrapped his arm around me. Everest pursed his lips. I sat with my leg bouncing and fingers tapping against my thighs. A headache was starting to erupt within me. Riona was glancing around, but her eyes were mainly on me. I wanted a few moments to breathe, but I wasn't going to get them. She was Marilyn's age. They looked similar, too.

She looked at me. "I'm sorry about your friend."

I nodded. "Thank you."

There was silence for a few moments before Everest spoke. "So, what's your plan?"

She took a breath. "I lived with him for fourteen years. I probably know him better than anyone else." She pulled out a dagger. "This blade has been charmed with a spell I invented. I infused elderberries into the metal. The concentration is so strong that one stab can kill him. It took me years to perfect it. I know how powerful he is, and this is our best chance."

Sampson nodded. "Sounds like it'll work."

Everest crossed his arms. "We'll leave tonight."

Riona smiled at me. I managed to give her a brief smile in return. All I could think about was wanting to eliminate Gregory. I wanted him to feel what Marilyn had felt. And when I watched the life leave his poisoned body, maybe I'd be able to have closure.

CHAPTER SIXTEEN
ESME
THEN AND NOW

I wore a pair of black pants, a brown woolen shirt, and a leather jacket. My heavy boots protected my feet from the chill forest floor, and my hair was pulled back in a long, messy braid. Even though I had tried to control them, my red curls still escaped their hold. My nose was chilly, and I was a little worried it might snow. The night felt ominous.

Sampson was beside me as we hiked through the woods. His eyes were dark as I watched the wheels in his brain. He was unusually silent, and I wondered why. There were so many possibilities. His normally relaxed expression had vanished. It made me uneasy. Was he worried this would end badly? I was, too.

Everest was right behind us. His footsteps were quiet as he walked over the twigs and dry, fallen leaves. I hadn't looked back to see his expression, but I imagined it was one of exhaustion. We were all worn down.

I was still trying to process the fact that they had a sister. Riona had literally appeared out of nowhere, but it was very convenient. Still, the whole idea seemed crazy. The boys had gained a sister out of thin air. All of a sudden, we had another member of this kamikaze-prone group. After what had happened to Marilyn, we would be lucky if we all survived. Still, every single one of us was determined to kill Gregory. He had hurt each of us in so many ways. Gregory had killed Riona's mother, kidnapped, poisoned, and murdered Marilyn, and tricked Sampson and Everest's mother into being with him. He was a murderous psychopath with a lack of empathy or capacity for decency. His actions in 1713 made me even more furious with him.

Riona was using a tracking spell to find Gregory. She had taken blood from herself, Everest and Sampson to start the process. They were his children, and DNA was needed to activate the tracking power. Now, we were following a black line that had appeared on a map of the area. It would show us where Gregory was.

She was more resourceful than any other sixteen-year-old I had encountered. Riona acted more like she was twenty than a teenager. She even looked older. Maybe all her time alone had matured her beyond her years. Her blue eyes were haunted. In that way, she resembled Everest. Maybe the siblings did have some things in common. The only connection they shared was a crazy father, but maybe they had more similarities than were obvious.

When we reached the end of the black line on the map, I looked up to examine our surroundings. We were nowhere particularly interesting. After our long walk, we were still in the woods. A little way ahead of us was a cabin that looked like it belonged in a painting. There was a chimney with smoke and the smell of freshly cooked steak flowing from the house. The only light was the soft illumination of a few lanterns that could be seen in the window. Of all the places to go, why would he choose here? Maybe he needed time to devise a plan, or he simply wanted a change of scenery. The little cabin was definitely more pleasant than the musty mansion he had vacated. Still, if I were him, I would have been on a plane by now. Of course, he must not have known much about modern society. He had been locked away for centuries.

"I've waited so long for this," Riona whispered.

Everest placed his hand on her shoulder. "Soon it'll be over."

Sampson sighed. "Yeah, we just have to figure out how to stab him first. No big deal. It's not like we failed terribly the last time we tried this."

"Who's taking the dagger?" I asked.

Everyone stood silently for a few moments. We all wanted to kill him, but only one of us could do it. It didn't really matter, though. No matter who wielded the dagger, he'd still end up with the poison in his body.

Riona handed the dagger to Sampson. "Here, you're the oldest."

He raised his eyebrows. "I'm not sure how relevant that is, but okay."

She shrugged. "He did cause the death of your daughter. In your past life, that is."

Sampson and I made hesitant eye contact while Everest looked at the ground. The tension had skyrocketed. This was still a topic we hadn't really delved into. Right now was not a great time to start family counseling. After all, we were attempting an assassination.

Riona tensed. "Oh, touchy subject."

"Let's just get to it," Everest said. "Sampson and I will go through the main part of the house to find him. Esme and Riona can follow. Try to find a back entrance, but be safe."

Riona nodded. "All right."

Sampson's hand brushed mine. Everest turned away from us with pain in his eyes. I felt a tinge of hurt in my heart. I wanted to go to him, but this wasn't the time to discuss our complex problems. Sampson placed his hand on the side of my face and leaned down to gently brush his lips against mine.

"In case anything happens...," he whispered.

I shook my head. "Nothing will."

He smiled softly before turning away to follow Everest toward the house. In the dark of night, they looked like shadows. I didn't like watching them go. The lack of their presence was so obvious. There was a sudden vacancy around me. I knew it was important, though. Gregory would have no idea we were coming. Our stealth and silencing charms made sure he wouldn't detect our presence.

"I see why you like my brothers," Riona whispered. "They both love you."

The air in my lungs seemed to evaporate. Love was such a strong word. Could they really feel so passionately for me? It had been hundreds of years since the first occurrence of our love triangle. Seventeen-thirteen was a long time ago. I barely knew anything of who I'd been. Cassandra seemed far away and close to me all at the same time. The three of us had been reunited less than a week ago. Was love really possible? I didn't know how I felt. There was so much conflict within me. I couldn't worry about it now, though.

"We should get going," I replied.

She nodded. "I'll follow you."

I pulled the twin machetes from my back before heading around the end of the house, Riona following me. I had learned how to use a number of weapons. Daggers were my preferred tools, but I was all right with these. Other than our encounter with Gregory, I had never actually participated in violence. Clearly, Sampson preferred a bow. When he held it in his hand, he looked stronger. It was like a natural extension of his body. Everest appeared best with a sword.

He held it as if it was meant to be in his hand.

For so long, our community had been under attack. Since the existence of our kind, we'd been in danger. Long before the invention of modern weapons, we had started training ourselves in the art of self-defense. Young witches and warlocks were taught magic, but they also learned how to fight in physical combat. In the twenty-first century, it was more of a tradition than a necessity. Still, the suspicion of attack was always there. It seemed to be stuck in our collective consciousness.

Riona was right behind me. She clutched her bow as if it were the only thing between her and death. Even with magic dancing on the tips of her fingers, the weapon made her feel safe. I understood that. The physical barrier of a weapon seemed different than the openness of magic. Even with all my spells, knives gave me a sense of safety.

Only a few moments into our surveying of the house, I heard a large crash on the second floor. Riona and I shared a nervous glance. Shouts began to pour through the windows. I wanted to be with them. Looking up, I noticed a large, circular window. It was on the second floor, but there was a tree right beside it. Without a second thought, I tucked my machetes back into their sheaths on my back. I stepped on the bottom branch and pulled myself up. A few seconds later, I was even with the window.

Looking inside, I saw Gregory pinned against the wall.

He was fighting, though. Sampson was physically restraining him, but he was having to endure a lot. Gregory kept whispering "dolor" while pressing his hands into Sampson. I knew the spell. When uttered with physical contact, it made the victim feel as if electricity was running through their bones. I could see the pain on Sampson's face. The dagger was strapped to his hip, but he couldn't release Gregory long enough to grab it. Everest was dodging the objects Gregory was telepathically throwing at him. I had no idea how to do that. Silent magic was something that took decades of careful concentration. Glass was crashing around Everest as sharp pieces flew through the air. Gregory knew more spells than I'd ever contemplated learning. Of course, having hundreds of years to fill provided lots of time for memorization.

The window was glass, but I didn't have time to worry about it. With a deep breath, I threw myself through the window and into the house. I felt the glass shatter around me, and pieces cut into my skin. The sting of cuts was everywhere. I could feel the adrenaline rushing within my chest. It was better than caffeine.

I vaguely heard Riona yell my name.

"Esme, I'm coming!" Riona shouted.

The ringing in my ears prevented me from responding. Instead, I focused on pulling myself to my feet. There was blood on the floor, probably mine. Everyone in the room was aware of my presence. I had literally come crashing into the room.

I looked at Gregory. "Ignis," I mumbled.

In a flash brighter than I'd expected, his body burst into flames. Sampson's face became covered in shock. Everest collapsed to the ground with a giant gash on his arm from where an object had been thrown at him. Before I had the chance to do anything, Gregory's eyes met mine. He was screaming as the flames climbed his form. I hated what I had just done. It was an unspoken taboo—witches didn't play with fire. We were far too familiar with its effects. I had just doomed a man to burn to death, and I was repulsed by it. Energy was draining from my body as I willed the spell to continue. It was one of the only times I'd used magic to hurt someone. Sampson didn't waste another moment before shoving the dagger into Gregory's chest.

"Relinquo," I whispered.

The fire vanished, and Gregory collapsed onto the floor, the dagger firmly planted in his heart. Sampson stood over him with a blank expression on his face. Gregory turned his head to face me. I barely had enough energy to stay on my feet. Creating the fire had worn me out; I wasn't used to using that much magic. I needed to work on my endurance.

"The key," he whispered. "You're the key."

I listened to him for a moment, wondering what he meant. Of course, I wanted to know. But I couldn't stop to think about it.

Everest, who had managed to stop the bleeding from the cut on his arm, walked over to stand beside me. "What do you mean?"

"She's the key to everything. She can release the gates," Gregory whispered.

Everest, Sampson, and I exchanged a look of confusion. Release the gates? The key? He was just crazy. It was probably his last attempt to drive us mad. I wouldn't pay attention to his mysterious claims. He had done nothing to make me trust him.

With a final agonized groan, Gregory's head fell against the floor. The poison had killed him in less than a minute. The burns covering his whole body certainly hadn't given him extra time. All his hair was gone, and his skin was oozing and bubbly. Riona had certainly fashioned an effective weapon. We had to be careful with it, though. It probably still had enough elderberry left to kill us. We would store it away for when we needed it.

Sampson reached down to close Gregory's eyes. Everest slipped his hand into mine and pulled me against him. I took a deep breath, inhaling the scent of his blood, sweat, and leather jacket. I had never been so relieved to inhale the odor of dried blood; it had stopped dripping from his arm. We were all okay, and I didn't have to bury anyone I loved today.

"Your arm, is it all right?" I asked.

He squeezed me tighter. "I'll be fine. I just got hit by a vase. It shattered against me."

I took a quick glance at his arm. Shards of pottery were still in his skin. I'd have to pull them out and clean his cut. We'd need a sanitizing potion.

"I made it!" Riona shouted as she climbed through the window.

I had forgotten she was a few inches shorter than me. She had probably had trouble pulling herself up from the lower branch. Sweat glistened on her forehead as she leaned against the wall. Her eyes were filled with surprise at the quiet scene.

"You're late to the party, blondie," Sampson mumbled.

"You killed him," Riona whispered.

"It wasn't easy," Sampson murmured.

We were all silent for a few minutes. Everest released me before tearing a piece of fabric and wrapping it around his arm. Riona walked over to help him. They wrapped it tightly to prevent dirt from entering his wound.

Sampson and I exchanged a look of exhaustion. He was hurt from the electrocution, but he wouldn't show it. I could see it in his eyes; he couldn't hide it there. I placed my hand on his arm and gave it a little squeeze. He smiled down at me before pulling me against him and placing a kiss on top of my head.

CHAPTER SEVENTEEN
ESME
THE POWERFUL ONE

The smell of cranberries and sugar wafted through the air, along with the scent of cinnamon and apples. In the frigid air outside my house, I shivered as I pulled my blanket tightly around me. It was chilly and wet, but the sky was pretty.

We had created a small campfire in the front yard. I didn't want to be inside when the moon was shining so brightly. Everest sat by the fire as he sprinkled the sugar over the popping fruits. His light eyes were focused as he performed his task with precision. His smile held warmth in its soft assurance of gentleness. I sighed as his messy hair fell into his face. He reached to pull it back into its hold, giving me a nice view of his chest. I smiled softly as my abdomen warmed. His gentle grace and elegant beauty would always be the most attractive part of his masculine form.

Sampson stood beside him, slicing cheese and vegetables. His shirt tightly gripped his biceps. I wanted to avert my eyes, but it was hard to. My stomach was turning upside down as I traced his chest, arms, and torso with my wide eyes. Somehow, I still wasn't accustomed to the sight of his body. The glow from the fire was illuminating his face in a way I couldn't turn away from. Before I had the chance to look down, his eyes met mine. There was a glimmer in them that made me bite my lip.

Riona was humming beside me as she cut the bread. Her blonde hair seemed to shimmer in the darkness like a heavenly being. Her cheeks were flushed from the chill, but her eyes were still the same icy blue. Riona was almost the perfect picture of beauty. Marilyn had been, too. They looked so much alike that it gave me a fondness for Riona. When I looked at her, I saw my best friend. Marilyn was gone, but she'd always be alive in my heart. And Riona, maybe I could be friends with her too.

"Riona," I whispered. "Gregory said something before you got there. As he was dying, he referenced something. He said that I was the key. Do you know anything about that? He seemed to have a message, not that I'm sure I would trust him."

She tensed for a moment. "I do. I know what he was talking about."

"Well, what is it?" I asked.

There was a moment of silence. She turned to meet my eyes before answering. "When I was growing up, Gregory was obsessed with Cassandra — with you. He was a talented warlock. In all his scheming and desperation, he did a lot of reading. He researched, studied, and read. I watched, never understanding his obsession. One day, I asked him why he was fascinated with you. He gave me an answer I never expected. Gregory told me there were prophecies foretelling your return. He said you would come back to the world, but he didn't know when. Eventually, he became convinced that signs were pointing to your return in this century. He did spells searching for you and was completely entranced when he finally figured out where you were. Gregory explained that you were what he described as the 'key to everything.' I began to think his obsession had finally driven him to insanity, but then he showed me the book. It was ancient."

We sat quietly for a few more minutes. I could tell she was taking her time, but the suspense was getting to me. I needed to know what it meant. There were so many things I didn't know about who I was. I was unsure of a lot, but I wanted to learn. It had become clear that my past was important to my future. I needed to know all the messy details from my former life.

"What did the book say?" I asked.

She continued. "The book was maybe from the sixteenth century, I'm not sure. It was before 1713. To me, it seemed as old as the earth. Many people would have ignored its contents. To the untrained eye, it might appear to be a poem or strange omen. But to me — to a witch — the meaning was clear. It spoke of 'the powerful one.' It said she would bring us back, raise us from the earth, and reunite us with life. That 'the powerful one' would save her own. You became a legend in my mind. The prophecy talked about you like you were some sort of fairytale being. You have power beyond anything the rest of us do."

I shook my head. "What is that supposed to mean?"

She let out a breath. "It means you'll bring them all back. You have the power to raise every single witch who has ever died. You're the key. Our people have been persecuted for over a thousand years, and you have the power to give the witches life again. Your power can give our people — our families and friends — a new opportunity."

I was stunned. Shock traveled through me as I processed the importance of her words. This was the most surprising thing I'd learned yet. I was Cassandra, the most powerful witch of all time, and I had the ability to raise thousands of witches from the dead. It had been done for individual people before. Sometimes a powerful group of witches and warlocks could bring a person back. It involved dark magic, though. I couldn't practice that. But this was different. It wasn't fueled by sacrifice or corrupt energy. My heart was lurching in my chest. So much rested upon my shoulders.

"Who all knows?" I whispered.

She sighed. "I'm not sure. It's not an easy discovery

to make, but I'm sure someone else was able to find the prophecy. There may be a couple of copies."

I took a moment to calm my thoughts. Everything seemed to be spinning. The world was once again shifting. My life seemed to be an endless maze of confusing twists and turns that led me to a field filled with perplexity. No matter how hard I tried, I couldn't go back. It was impossible for me to ignore who I was. Glancing back at Sampson and Everest, I saw my past and future blend together.

"Are you all right?" Riona asked.

I looked back at her, the sister of the most important men in my life, and sighed. "Yes. As all right as I can be, anyway."

She nodded. "I get it. Trust me, I've been amazed by your abilities for years."

We sat in silence for a few more minutes. Eventually, Sampson made his way over to us. Everest was still focused on his task. I watched him as he placed the fruit into a large bowl. He smiled as he sprinkled cinnamon on top of it.

"What's wrong? You look like you've had the energy sucked out of you," Sampson said.

He sat down and wrapped his arm around my back. His other hand rested on my thigh as I leaned into him. I felt the heat of his skin, the firmness of his chest, and the warmth of his fingers against me. With a small smile, I rested my head on his shoulder. He squeezed me tight against him as if the world depended on our embrace.

"Riona, will you tell him what you told me?" I asked.

She nodded, beckoned Everest over, and began recounting her story. Both men were silent as they listened. When she got to the final part, I felt Sampson's muscles tense against my body. Everest's face was covered by a mask of concentration I couldn't seem to look away from. He met my eyes and smiled lightly. Looking back into his glimmering crystal eyes, I smiled too.

"What does it mean?" Sampson asked.

Riona's eyes met mine. "I hope it means you'll do the spell. Other than killing Gregory, it's the reason I came to find you. You're Cassandra, the powerful one, and I need your help."

I made eye contact with Everest. He was still silent in a state of focus. I could practically see the questions drifting through his mind. Sampson was watching me. His body was still stiff as he pulled me closer. It was a few moments before I realized I was supposed to respond.

I looked down at my hands. "I don't know."

She looked at me in desperation. "Please, Esme. This could bring so much happiness to our lives. Your mother could come back. You'd get to see Marilyn. My mom would be alive again."

I took a deep breath. "I need to think about it."

She nodded. "All right, I'll give you time."

We ate the rest of our meal in silence.

Chapter Eighteen
Esme
"Grass Is Greener"

Sleep took me away from the night and transported me to a dark void. Instead of the warm blankets that had surrounded me, I was wrapped in a silver dress that seemed to be made of my own energy. My hair was hanging down my back like a red wave of ruby curls. The floor beneath me shimmered like black glass covered by a blanket of ice. The area seemed to hold a million stars but also felt beyond time and space. It was like a void but prettier than expected. The air was neither hot nor cold but almost water-like. My movements were slow and fluid.

The voices started as nothing more than whispers. At first, I could barely hear them. Their soft words sounded like a breeze. They drifted by me like pollen in the spring. Yet as I waited, they became louder. They gradually grew until I felt as if the room were ringing. Echoes, shouts, and screams were all around me. I wanted to cover my ears, but nothing worked. The voices grew louder than anything I'd ever heard. Eventually, the pain was so intense I started to cry.

All of a sudden, the voices stopped. The room was once again silent. But when I opened my eyes, I was no longer in the star-filled blackness. Instead, shades of gold were swirling around me to create a tunnel that disappeared in the distance. I saw a soft light at the end. Before I could process what I was doing, I started running. I was desperate to escape the emptiness left by the former voices. There was no doubt in my mind that it was a dream, but the pain was no less intense.

When I reached the end of the tunnel, I passed through a little portal of glowing light. Time seemed to stop for a moment, and I felt like I couldn't breathe. My lungs were restricted, but it only lasted less than a second.

As I took another step, the light disappeared. The sun was pouring down on me in a field filled with flowers. Butterflies drifted by as the wind ushered them along. Looking down, I noticed a simple dress made of animal skins that fell just above my knee. A necklace of seashells hung down to my chest. Reaching up to touch my hair, I realized that it had been pulled back in a braid that fell below my hips. There was nothing but grass, trees, flowers, and sunlight around me.

After walking a bit through the woods, I smelled the familiar scent of smoke. I followed it to find a group of witches huddled around a campfire, a potion boiling atop it. It was an old, simple one I'd learned when I was young. Just some herbs and a few flower petals used to create a sleeping aid. It was so safe that it could be administered to babies or young children who were sick. The women were all dressed like me. I didn't know where or when I was, but it was certainly a long time ago. The dream was taking place much earlier than 1713. This place looked to be somewhere in Europe long before the rise of Greece or Rome. These women were tribal, hunter-gatherer people. I couldn't understand their language, but I knew it was some form of unique dialect. They clearly couldn't see me. It seemed as if I were a spirit floating among them. I'd never had a dream like this before. It wasn't a memory. From what I could tell, the scene was a historical event I'd never witnessed.

There was a little shout as two girls ran by. They were maybe four or five, with dark brown hair and deep chocolate eyes. Their pink lips parted in smiles as they laughed. I watched with a bubbly happiness in my chest. They reminded me of Marilyn and I when we were little. Two little girls with simple happiness; it was beautiful.

Large tents were positioned in an oval around the fire. Women were cleaning nuts, cutting fruit, and sewing garments. Their hair was contained in braids or pulled back with leather wraps. The air was peaceful with the cries of babies, talking of children, and whispers of women speaking in calm tones. I watched with fascination as an older woman recounted a tale to a group of toddlers. They listened with eager ears as her voice rose and fell during the adventurous story.

Two warlocks emerged from a tent. The first approached two women sitting side-by-side. One was heavily pregnant, while the other held a small boy on her lap. They both had blonde hair pulled back in cornrows. He reached down and placed soft kisses on each of the women's lips. I immediately understood. Polygamy had never been particularly common among witches and warlocks, but it hadn't been rare in ancient times. The women were always respected, though. Instead of the men choosing their wives, two women, most likely friends, would decide to bring a man into both of their lives. The three of them looked perfectly content together. With a wave of the warlock's hand, two daisies sprouted from the ground in front of the women. He lifted both and placed one in each of their laps. They smiled up at him with love in their eyes.

The other warlock walked to a little girl, who hugged his legs and jumped into his arms. A young woman walked up and wrapped her arms around him. He leaned in and inhaled the scent of her hair. An older woman, maybe sixty or seventy, watched them with contentment. A happy little family. The sight of them brought a lightness to my heart.

Suddenly a group of men, tall and dressed in animal skins, emerged from the woods. In their hands were wooden bows, and arrows were strapped to their backs. The witches and warlocks froze. Moments later, the leader of the intruding group walked forward. No one was sure what to do. A witch with a round, pregnant belly approached him. He leaned in and looked at her with angry eyes. The man must have been the human father of her child.

"Hexe," he whispered.

She looked up at him, attempting to touch his face, but he swatted her away. The warlocks began to approach, but with a quick, fluid motion, the man shoved a spear through her chest.

I screamed, but no one could hear me. I was as helpless as the very air around us. The children were crying, women screaming, and warlocks fighting. While the mothers attempted to run into the woods with their children, the two warlocks tried to hold the men off, but there were too many attackers for it to matter. They were outnumbered. There were at least ten men within the barbaric pack. With another quick strike, the first warlock was struck to the ground. He began coughing up blood. While his second wife grabbed her son and rushed away, the first collapsed next to him with heart-wrenching sobs. One of the men grabbed her, pulling her away from her dying husband.

While some of the men mercilessly killed the witches, others grabbed the young women and began pulling them away. The older witch, who had been telling the story to the children, stood and raised her hands. Fire erupted from the ground, but it didn't last long. As soon as an arrow pierced her, she fell to the earth. Her magic died along with her.

I watched the scene in horror as the screams echoed around me. Pulling my hands to my ears, I tried to block out the sounds. I couldn't, though. They seemed to be coming from within my own mind.

Moments later, the noises began to fade. When I opened my eyes, all I saw was darkness.

With panic inside my body, I drifted away into a sound, dreamless sleep. I knew it wouldn't be restful, yet I was glad for the stillness. There was horror in my mind. When I woke, their screams would resonate within my soul.

Everest

As soon as I closed my eyes, I saw light. I was dreaming... again. Sighing in annoyance, I began to glance around. The glaring brightness gently softened to a dim glow that seemed to come from somewhere above me. Looking ahead, I saw a door, gold with an amethyst handle. With nowhere else to go, I approached it.

As soon as I stepped through the door, I began walking on a glass floor. For a moment, I was worried I would fall. Above me was an endless expanse of darkness with the sweet smell of flowers. It was open and cool. Somewhere in the far distance, I saw a galaxy of purple, blue, and green. I didn't know what it was, but it was beautiful.

Looking down, I glimpsed a heartwarming scene. There was a beach, ocean, and golden sunset. Dolphins floated in the waves, and seagulls soared overhead. A group of women and children rested upon the sand. Within the water, men lifted babies above the waves to watch the glimmer below. A little way back from the beach, an orchard filled with fruit trees led to a clearing decorated with sunflowers.

The people below were at peace. They were witches and warlocks who'd found contentment after death. A small smile spread across my lips. They were happy, and there was hope for the future. Where had Sampson, Esme, and I been for three centuries? Had we been at peace? Had we chosen to come back? I had no memory of this place or anywhere like it. Perhaps there was some happiness buried within my mind. That made hope spring up within my chest.

There was a place where flowers never stopped blooming. The lavender was a bright purple that reflected the sunlight. Cherries hung from the healthy trees. The air was always warm enough, and no one ever became sick. The people — my people — were happy. It was paradise and beauty. This place, whatever it was, gave the people below a chance to love without fear. One day, I hoped to join them. With one last look at the happy gathering, I closed my eyes.

Sampson

When I closed my eyes, a sensation of ice overwhelmed my body as if I had been shoved into a frozen wasteland. My face felt cold and strained. When I opened my eyes, I was met with a darkness that came over the frozen cave I seemed to inhabit. It was like I was standing inside an ice cube.

Looking around, I saw movement within the chill blocks. As I walked, my feet slid on the ice. I had to focus to steady myself — it was hard to balance. I paid intense attention to the little motions shrouded within the fragmented ice. There were shadows within, and they seemed alive. Moving closer, I saw something I had never expected.

A baby girl, wrapped in a white shawl, lay tucked within the frozen cube. I placed my hand against the icy encasement. For a moment, I panicked. How was she alive? Was she okay? She was so small. Her red hair and freckled cheeks made my mouth curve at the edges. I glanced at her tiny fingers and toes. My heart began pounding with protectiveness. Something in me knew before my brain had begun to process the imagery.

Before my eyes, she began to transform. I watched as she grew from an infant to a toddler, a child to a teen. At about the age of fourteen, her growth stopped. Her cherry-red lips, curly fire-like hair, and pale skin reminded me of Esme. They were different, though. Her hips were smaller, and her head more oval-shaped.

I was filled with awe. There was magic surrounding us. I had no idea where I was — I could only focus on the incredible aspects of this mystery location. Yes, it was a dream. Perhaps it was a metaphor, or maybe it was real. Either way, there was truth in the image.

For a moment, I stood in confusion. But after a second of understanding, I froze. She looked like Esme, yet she had my nose, high cheekbones, and long legs. The young teenage girl had transformed before my eyes. She was my daughter. The little girl that had died in the same fire in which we had perished in 1713. She was my baby. This was somewhere beyond the mortal world. She had grown up without us. My little girl — my princess — was alive. I could barely process the concept. My daughter had grown up in some icy encasement. I had no idea how it was possible or why. But the universe had decided that my daughter needed another chance. And if Esme brought the witches back, she would come with them.

We could have a family. This was our chance. I had to convince her this was the right choice. So many witches would be saved — our daughter would come back. She didn't deserve to be stuck in this ice cube forever. I wanted her to witness a sunset, see flowers, and taste the most delicious foods. My baby girl deserved to see the world. I would take her to the most beautiful oceans and charming valleys. This was the right thing, and I would be sure to do whatever I could to bring my little girl home. She belonged with us. And when we had her back, she would learn just how much she was loved. And then, Esme would truly choose me.

CHAPTER NINETEEN
ESME
GENEVA HOPE

I heard footsteps behind me as I rested on a tree stump a little way from the house. The soft moss was squishy beneath me. It was foggy outside, and the chill air fluttered around me like a river of snowflakes. I could barely see the sun, yet I had no want for its presence. The sweater provided warmth as I tugged it around me. Its woolen length wrapped me in a layer of heat. My hair was bunched in a braid at the back of my head, and my lips were slightly parted as I inhaled the dew-filled morning air.

After seventeen years of my current life, I had never grown tired of the fog. It drifted up from the river like a blanket of gentle droplets. I was filled with a sense of calm when I walked through it. It reminded me of natural comfort and beauty. I didn't know if I had loved it in my past life or if this was a new fascination. Either way, it was part of who I'd become.

I had come to realize that my soul was divided. I was a witch, a woman, a best friend, and a power figure. No matter how much I tried to ignore it, I was Cassandra. But despite that, I was also Esme. Two worlds collided to create the woman I was. Reality was outside my control. It might have been easier if I'd never known of my life in 1713. But then again, I wouldn't want to give up Sampson and Everest.

When I woke after the dreams, I was covered in sweat. After lathering my body in soap and trying to wash the terror away, I came outside and found my way to this stump. It was still early morning, and the cool breeze was clearing my mind. I could barely feel my fingers, but at least I no longer heard the screams of the dead.

I didn't turn at the sound of Sampson's footsteps. I knew it was him. He walked differently than Everest. Sampson's footsteps were heavy and strong. Everest walked with a more nimble pattern. Sampson placed his hand on my back and laid a soft kiss on the top of my head. I leaned into him and felt the hardness of his abdomen behind me.

"I was worried about you," he whispered.

I nodded. "I just needed some space."

He sat beside me and placed his hand on my knee. I closed my eyes as a tear dripped down my face. No matter where I went, the nightmares from only hours ago kept invading my mind. Sampson didn't know what I had experienced. I saw the horror some of our people had suffered.

I couldn't describe it to him because being there made it feel real.

Seeing things were different than reading about them. History books couldn't always tell the small details. Cries of pain couldn't be written down the way they could be heard. I witnessed it last night. Their faces were still in my mind. I might never forget how they screamed in fear for their lives.

"I had a dream last night," he said.

I turned toward him with anticipation. Had he seen the same thing? Had we witnessed the same tragedy? If we had, perhaps I could share my pain. He reached up to touch my face, and I rested my head against his palm. We sat in silence for a few moments.

There were many words I could have used to describe our relationship. It was complicated, yes. We had many feelings toward each other that were hard to put into words. But after our time together, I no longer wanted to deny that my heart beat faster when he glanced at me. When our fingers touched, I felt warm and tight. My abdomen twisted when his arms wrapped around me. I wasn't sure how he felt, but our eye contact told me enough. There was love. I truly, innately loved him. No matter how the love was interpreted or what we did with it, there was no denying its impact on me.

"Tell me about it," I replied.

He took a deep breath. "In any of your visions, have you seen her? Our daughter."

I had a sharp intake of breath. We had never discussed this. The topic had been buried in a pile of issues to be talked about when our lives weren't in danger. I didn't want to talk about her this morning. All I could think about was how she must have died. I hadn't been able to save her. After three hundred years, it felt so recent. She had been on my mind since I learned of my identity. It didn't matter that I had no idea what she looked like—I knew she was mine. My soul knew just how much I missed her. I had thought about how much she must have weighed, what her eyes had looked like, and what she had sounded like after she was born. The knowledge that I couldn't see her was like a deep, bloody wound that had been ripped open and was bleeding all over my mind.

I shook my head. "No."

He smiled. "I did."

Confusion traveled through me. My head was spinning with shock. My stomach turned upside down, and it seemed I couldn't find oxygen. I suddenly felt my vision grow blurry, and I tried to hold myself up. Why had he seen her, but I hadn't? It wasn't fair. I was shocked, almost to the point of throwing up.

Sampson wrapped me in his arms and pulled me against him. I breathed in the scent of his shirt. Placing my hands against his hard chest, I felt my heart rate slow. I pushed into him as much as I could. My thoughts were spinning, yet all I wanted was to feel him.

"Tell me about her," I whispered.

I could feel him sigh. "She's beautiful. Her hair is like yours. I could barely believe it when I saw how much she looked like you. She was what I'd imagined her to be."

I looked up at him. "Where was your dream? She died as a baby."

He nodded. "I know. This was different, though. I was somewhere beyond. I'm not sure if it was a metaphor or a truly mystical place, but she was there. I watched her body grow from an infant to a teenage girl. She was frozen in ice. It was as if time had stopped, and she was the real Sleeping Beauty. I wanted to hold her so badly, Esme."

I bit my lip in sudden understanding. My dream made so much more sense. Sampson and I had witnessed connected visions. They weren't exactly the same, yet they communicated similar messages. Our daughter could come back. We had the power to bring her back to life. I could truly have the chance to love her. Sampson and I would be able to give her a family. That was what she deserved. I didn't feel old enough to be a mother, but I was around the same age in this life as I had been in my last when she was born.

She wasn't the only one I could bring back, though. Marilyn was out there, too. If I brought the witches back, she could live a happy life. I wanted to watch her experience the things she had dreamed of. It's what she deserved. If I performed the spell, I'd have my best friend and my daughter back. Maybe that would really give me peace.

There were others, too. My mom was on the other side. So many witches would be brought back. For a moment, I thought of what it would be like. I would meet my daughter, whom I had no memory of. We wouldn't know each other, but we could grow to. I could give her back the life Gregory had stolen.

Yet it wasn't that simple. Not all witches were good. Like any group of people, there were evil ones among us. I might bring back murderers, abusers, and all other types of villainous individuals. I didn't want to be blamed for that. They could cause absolute chaos. Harm could come to people if I decided to perform the spell. What if I became the reason someone ended up dead? I might become a villain.

Why did I have the power to do this? I didn't want it. I suddenly understood why queens felt burdened. Too much responsibility fell upon them. We didn't volunteer for it. It's not like I'd signed up. There had been no questions about whether or not I wanted the power to bring witches back from the dead. I had no desire to hold this much responsibility.

"Esme?" Samson whispered.

"I have to think," I mumbled.

Before he could reply, I stood and ran off into the fog.

When I reached the top of the hill, I stopped running. I had dashed all the way through the forest, up the smallest black hill, and into the rocky regions, where I could overlook the nearby valley. From there, I could witness the fog covering the ground below. It had taken me at least thirty minutes to reach the place I remembered. Marilyn and I had sometimes come up here when we were younger. The rosewood trees were so pretty that she used to bring a sketchbook with her and outline them. When we went back home, she would use her drawing to help her recall their branches and leaves. It helped her with the paintings she spent so much time on.

Sitting upon the rocks, I could imagine her beside me. It was as if I could feel her presence. Perhaps in some way, she was with me. Marilyn and I were so connected that nothing could truly pull us apart. Her memory was alive. That alone gave me a sense of comfort. I wanted her back, but I wasn't sure what to do. The decision felt so heavy. Thousands of lives were in my hands. I controlled whether they came back to life or not. It was a burden I would have gladly gifted to Riona — she seemed eager for it. At least that way, it wouldn't be my job.

I felt guilty for running away from Sampson. My boots were covered in mud, and my heart was pounding. It had been a choice my instincts made. I knew I needed to be alone, but I still felt his loss like an ache in my body. Having him gone was like losing a puzzle piece. Nothing seemed to work properly without him by my side. Still, I needed to think. I didn't want to talk, not when I was the only one responsible for making the choice. If something terrible resulted from it, they wouldn't be blamed. It would be me who would suffer the guilt.

Suddenly, my mind became fuzzy. A terrible headache was coming on. Not surprising considering that I now held the power of life within my grasp. I'd gone from a high-profile witch to the angel of death in a matter of moments. There were probably others who knew of my ability. The thought made a shiver run through my body. It was common knowledge that I was Cassandra. If Gregory had been able to discover my power, others probably knew. It was a choice I would make in front of thousands. I was now a leader, though I had never desired to be. Being Cassandra made me royalty. I was practically a queen, and the crown was too heavy. My love life was no longer my most pressing problem. And considering how complicated my romantic relationships were, that was a pretty big deal.

I closed my eyes for a moment. The headache dulled, but I was astounded when I opened my eyes. The world had turned black and white, literally. There was no color within sight. Biting my lip, I felt frustration rise within me. I was tired of these memory/dream visions that seemed to invade my mind every chance they could. It was irritating. I wanted one moment of calm. I couldn't tell what this was — after all, I wasn't asleep. This was something different.

I heard a rustling behind me and turned around. A

small gasp escaped as I lifted my hand to cover my mouth. Marilyn was standing behind me, her pretty blonde hair almost translucent. She wore a white dress that fell to her knees. It was plain cotton but highlighted her little figure in a gorgeous way. I wondered if she was a figment of my imagination for a moment. She was otherworldly beautiful. But when she opened her arms, I knew she was real.

I dashed to her and wrapped my arms around her neck. When she hugged me back, I burst into tears. I hadn't been sure if we'd ever meet again. She felt solid in my arms. It was as if she was truly alive.

"How?" I asked.

She smiled at me. "You're on the border between the physical world and the spiritual one. Don't worry. You're still alive. You just seem to have an odd habit of shifting to this side of the metaphysical line when you get stressed. I've been watching it happen for days."

I rolled my eyes at her playful smile. "Trust me, I'm not choosing to do it."

She giggled. "I know, but maybe it'll give us a few chances to see each other."

I pursed my lips. "Is this black and white version of the world where you are all the time?"

She shook her head. "No, it's in between both dimensions. But because I'm a witch, I can choose to come here. It's how I watch you."

I glanced around. "Where are you normally?"

"A beautiful place," she replied with a sparkle in her eyes. "My mom is there, and so is yours. There are witches and warlocks all around. Humans are there, too. It's like a garden of happiness. The other side is filled with nature, light, and peace. I'm happy."

There was a moment of calm silence. "You like it there?"

She nodded. "Very much. I could choose to be reborn if I wanted to, but I'm content. I might even fall in love. There are lots of warlock boys."

I smiled. "Good, I'm glad you're happy."

She paused for a moment. "Someone's coming. It's better if you're back in your human body. Don't worry. I'll be watching you."

I felt her begin to fade away. "I love you!"

She gave me a final smile. "I love you, too."

When I opened my eyes, the world was once again filled with life.

"Esme?" Everest whispered.

There was a moment before I answered. "Yes?"

He sat a few inches away from me. The fog was starting to fade, and the sun was pouring through the sky. Flowers were sprouting from the ground below. I took a moment to admire the soon arrival of spring. Everything seemed brighter, more pleasant. Purple, blue, and yellow were blooming around me. Lilacs had always made my heart flutter. They were starting to erupt all over the hill. The rosewood trees were my favorite, though.

"Sampson told me what happened," he said.

I nodded. "He probably thinks I'm crazy."

He shook his head. "No, he was just worried he might have really upset you."

I looked down. "I'm overwhelmed."

There was a brief pause before he placed his hand over mine. "I can't imagine how difficult it is. As much as I'm frustrated with my position in this family, yours is the hardest. I can't forget that."

I nodded. "It's not easy."

He squeezed my hand. "I'm sorry I haven't been supportive enough."

Our eyes met, and at that moment, I saw something. He was in love with me. I could tell he was trying to hide it, but his lapis-blue eyes couldn't conceal his feelings. There was a tenderness that erupted within me. I thought of Sampson, but my concern quickly faded.

He turned away. "Esme, now is not the time. No matter what you decide to do about Sampson and me, you have bigger concerns. We can talk about this when there's not a world-changing choice to be made."

I laughed. "I'm not sure our lives will ever be peaceful again. It seems that chaos follows us."

Everest shook his head. "I won't be the one to pull you away from your duty. No matter how you feel about yourself, you are our queen...my queen."

"I'm only a girl," I whispered.

He ran his thumb across my cheek while his eyes traveled down my form. "One who's stolen my heart."

I ran my hand through his long blond hair. "Though I've tried, I can't seem to understand my own feelings. Lines aren't clear, and I'm not sure where I belong."

He began to move away. "I understand."

I grabbed his arm. "No. I haven't committed to anyone. They can call me whatever they like. The people can criticize me. But until I've decided, I intend to act on how I feel. And in moments like this, my base instincts make it clear. I know there's a part of my soul that loves you. I feel the same way about Sampson, though."

There was a second pause before he wrapped his arms around me and tugged me toward him. I hadn't expected it. Everest was always so passive. But when his hands found my hips and pulled me close, I lost myself in his lips. The curve of his shoulder and the strength of his chest pulled me in. Everest had the most curved jaw and gentle smile I had ever seen upon a man. His newly shaved cheeks were soft as I ran my fingers across them.

"You don't know how badly I've wanted to do that," he whispered.

CHAPTER TWENTY
ESME
BRIDGE

"What do you mean you've decided not to bring them back?" Riona shouted.

I looked at her with a calm expression. "The people on the other side are at peace. Thousands of witches are now with their families. It is not for me to decide whether or not they return to their physical bodies."

Everest gently placed his hand on my back. Sampson, who stood with his arms crossed, shot angry glances at him. I attempted to ignore them both as I reasoned with her. Riona had not taken the news well. She was furious. In her mind, I was practically stealing her mother from her. For some reason, Riona had been sure I would bring them back. Now that I had decided against it, she was beyond frustrated.

"It's not that I don't want to bring them back," I murmured. "I would love to meet my daughter. Ever since I found out that I was—am—Cassandra, I've wanted to hold her. I have thought about her every single day and will continue to do so until I die."

Riona shook her head. "You clearly don't care for Geneva. Yes, that's her name. You didn't even bother to learn it."

My heart became filled with anger. "Don't you dare accuse me of not caring for my daughter!"

"If you cared, you'd bring Geneva back," Riona hissed.

Sampson stepped between us. "I think de-escalating this situation may be the best temporary plan."

Riona shoved past him. "No. I helped you kill Gregory. You would have never accomplished it without me. I want my mom back, and you owe it to me."

I took a step away from her. "Riona, calm down. I want Marilyn back. She's my best friend. And there isn't a single moment my heart doesn't ache for the opportunity to meet my daughter. But if they're at peace, I don't want to take them away from that." There were a few moments of silence. "I saw Marilyn; she spoke to me. The spiritual world is filled with peace. She told me she was happy. I'm more than willing to bet your mom is, too."

She shook her head. "You don't understand. The spell gives them the ability to return to the physical world. It doesn't force them back into their mortal bodies. They can stay where they are if they want to. Yet if the witches desire to come back, they can. The spell is complex. It's a powerful prophecy. You're the only one with the chance to bring it to life. You can give them a chance to live the lives they never could."

Everest was entirely silent. "What's wrong?" I asked.

"I had a dream, as well," he replied. "I saw witches and warlocks at peace. They were happy together."

Sampson looked between us. "At the moment, I'm agreeing with Riona. I understand your point, Everest. But I want to meet my daughter, and this is my chance."

"What about the evils I could cause? If I do this, I could bring murderers, serial killers, and all kinds of sick, perverse criminals back to life. They would jump at the chance to live again. I don't think they'd simply sit back and let it pass," I replied.

Sampson gently took my hand in his. "That wouldn't be your fault. You can't control the actions of anyone else."

I looked into his eyes. "But it is my responsibility. The burden of guilt would belong to me."

Riona was frustrated. "We can't deny life from innocents simply to prevent the return of a few evil individuals we could simply eliminate. Please, Esme."

I grimaced. "I don't want to become a monster. I hate the idea of killing. It makes me sick. Sometimes it's necessary, but when we have the opportunity to choose peace, that's what I prefer. In the end, this is my decision."

Everest pulled me toward him. "This is entirely your

decision. But no matter what you decide, it will not make you a monster. You could never be that, Esme. You're a good person."

I looked between the three of them. So many emotions were coursing through me. Guilt and terror were creating a sense of dread within my stomach. I felt queasy and lightheaded. Why did this choice have to belong to me? I didn't want this.

Sampson was looking at me with pleading eyes. He wanted Geneva back. What he didn't know was that I ached for our daughter, too. She had died in a gruesome way. She was a victim of Gregory, possibly the most innocent victim of all. She deserved life. I wanted her to fall in love and be happy. Sampson was desperate for our chance to bring her back. He wanted our daughter with us again, and I understood his desire. I loved her more than I knew possible. It had been hundreds of years since I'd given birth to her, but it felt as if she'd been torn from me yesterday. His eyes were filled with unspoken yearnings. I watched as the pain became etched over his face. My heart twisted with the guilt of denying him. It was so odd to feel so much for someone I'd never met. But I imagined that if I became pregnant, it would be the same. Geneva was my daughter. My soul recognized our connection—she was a part of me.

Riona's eyes held anger and impatience. She wanted her mother back. It was understandable. She felt like I owed it to her. I couldn't deny that she'd helped us, and I'd always be thankful. She had not only been a great help but also a friend. I didn't want to lose the relationship between us because of this. It certainly wasn't my place to divide her from the brothers she barely knew. Up until a few days ago, they hadn't known she existed. Riona had been waiting for years to meet them. She wanted a family, and I couldn't criticize her for such a pure desire. I had the same one.

Everest stood behind me with a comforting smile on his face. The looks we shared felt almost scandalous. They were the type of looks only couples understood. I could read the unspoken words within his eyes as he encouraged me with the soft presence of his fingers upon my back. He was the only one out of the three of them who would accept my decision without putting up a fight. Everest valued my independence. He wanted to lift me up without shackling me to his own personal wants. Like Marilyn, he was truly very selfless. I had never met a man like him before.

Suddenly, a vibration shook the house. It felt like an earthquake but was not the result of natural causes. There was magic everywhere; I could feel the energy. The shakes were so strong that Riona lost balance and began to tumble toward the ground, but Sampson caught her and pulled her back up. Everest grabbed me before reaching to secure us through his hold on a built-in bookshelf.

After a few moments of unsettling vibrations, the

motions ceased. We all looked at each other in confusion.

"Cassandra!" three voices shouted.

Sampson rolled his eyes. "What now?"

I dashed to the door with the three of them right behind me. Without pausing, I stepped outside. When I looked in front of me, I was met with the sight of three middle-aged women with dark skin and heaps of curly black hair. Their eyes were a mysterious gray with speckles of gold. With such similar appearances, they must have been sisters. Their combined power was so strong I could feel it pulsing around me. Sampson, Everest, and Riona seemed to feel it, too. I exchanged a worried glance with them before turning back to the women.

The first one smiled. "Cassandra, a pleasure. My name is Sarah, and these are my sisters, Mary and Alyssa. We are the Sages."

With little compassion in my voice, I asked, "What do you want? You just about knocked my house to the ground."

Sarah smiled. "Well, let's get right to the point. A strong girl, I like you. My sisters and I have been watching you since your identity was revealed."

"That's not creepy," Sampson grumbled.

Sarah gave him an annoyed smile. "We wish for you to fulfill your duty in bringing the witches back to life."

"Get in line," I murmured under my breath.

Mary stepped forward. "Our sister is trapped in the

afterlife. We've tried to raise her but have been unsuccessful. We would like your help."

Alyssa nodded. "If you do not agree to assist, we will have to resort to...less pleasant forms of negotiation."

Riona put her hands on her hips. "What is the deal with violence? Was no one around here ever taught to say please and thank you?"

I gave a small smile. Though Riona and I disagreed about the right choice in this matter, it seemed we would always be on the same side. We weren't going to turn our backs on each other. We would argue, scream, and storm off. But after all of it, we would kill to keep each other safe. I'd known her for so little time, but I trusted her immensely. Riona and I were very different, yet practically sisters. She would never abandon me. Apparently, planning an assassination together created that kind of bond.

Sarah looked in her direction. "We wish you no harm. Like you, we simply wish to be reunited with the one we love."

I sighed. "Unfortunately, I've decided not to perform the spell."

Riona groaned. "Your stubbornness is going to kill all of us one day."

I gave her a sideways look, and she playfully rolled her eyes. She was willing to fight for me, even if she thought my choice was stupid. We shared a few moments of understanding eye contact. I could trust her.

Everest and Sampson stepped up beside me. "If you hurt her, it won't end well for you," Everest said.

Mary smiled. "Your confidence is charming, yet misguided. I do admire your chivalry, though. It's refreshing."

Sampson smirked. "Every time someone has told me that, they've always been wrong. I don't like losing. And considering I just killed my own murderous father, I think you might be underestimating my resolve. "

Riona rolled her eyes while Everest dismissed his comment. The Sages were quiet as everyone waited for me to speak. I didn't want to seem weak. If I obeyed every command I was given, I would seem like a weapon rather than a powerful witch. These women wanted to barge into my house and order me around. I wouldn't allow them to control me.

"No," I whispered. "I won't do it."

Faster than I could comprehend, Sampson, Everest, and Riona had knives against their throats. My hand flew to my mouth as I watched the Sages lock them into place. It had happened so fast that I couldn't stop it. I'd never expected them to act so harshly. All of this was apparently for love.

"You may be powerful, Cassandra, yet even your magic won't be able to save all three of them at the same time. If you refuse to perform the spell, you'll have to choose one to live while the others die. The only way they all survive is if you agree to do what we've already asked," Sarah said.

Everest's blue eyes were piercing through me. His face was neutral yet shrouded by fear. He didn't want to make me feel obligated. It scared me that he honored my freedom so much that he would be willing to sacrifice his life for it. I could never let him do that. He wouldn't become a martyr for me.

Tears were streaming down Riona's face. Her eyes were squeezed shut as pained sobs escaped her shaking body. The knife was so close to piercing her skin that it made me feel nauseous. She was sixteen, the same age Marilyn had been when she was murdered. Never again would I let another young girl die because of me. I wanted to protect her. After learning that my daughter had died in 1713 and watching the life leave my best friend, I wanted to protect every child I could.

Sampson appeared calm, but I could feel his anxiety. I could read the words in his body language. His open lips and tight shoulders reflected fear. Though he would never admit it, he was scared of death. He wasn't the type of man to cower or loosen his pride, but I knew he was fearful. I could see his inward anxiety. After what had happened in our past lives, I couldn't let him down again. Just because he was willing to give up his life didn't mean I would let him. I had a choice, too.

I had to be stronger than I had ever been before. No

matter my principles against forced cooperation or my naturally rebellious nature, I wouldn't let anyone die for me. This life would be different. We wouldn't be sacrificed because I refused to allow it. These people were my family, and I would protect them. I would not let them die, even if it meant sacrificing my conviction. I didn't have that type of nature. Selflessness wasn't my specialty.

"Let them go, and I'll do it," I whispered.

Alyssa nodded. "We appreciate your help."

With a synchronized flash, the Sages dropped their knives and stepped back. Sampson rushed toward me while Everest pulled a still sobbing Riona into his arms. There were a few trickles of blood dripping down her neck.

Sarah looked toward Riona. "Ms. Silverstone, I believe you have the spell?"

With shaking hands, Riona pulled it from her pocket. The paper was old and crinkly. It looked as if it had been stained by coffee and folded a hundred times. Her hands were weak as she handed it to me.

After reading it, I knew exactly what to do. It wasn't complicated at all. In fact, it was a rather simple yet draining spell. Yet, for some bizarre, mystical reason I truly didn't understand, I was the only one who could perform it. Riona had told me it was because no one had access to as much energy as I did. She claimed my connection to the spiritual world was stronger than most. No matter the answer, fate seemed to enjoy throwing curveballs right at me.

I lifted my hands toward the evening sky as the energy vibrated around me. It was terrifying. Before I even started speaking, my eyes fluttered shut. I could feel my blue dress fluttering in the air flowing around me like a tornado of power. My red hair became a current of fire flowing behind me as my face tilted toward the sun. When I opened my mouth, my fingertips came alive. I felt the entire force of nature behind me. It was exhilarating yet intimidating. It was almost like an out-of-body experience. I hardly knew where I ended, and the energy began.

As I lifted my palms toward the sky, words began to stream from my mouth. "Surge Sursus, surge sursus, surge sursus!"

My eyes flew open as silver streams of light began flowing from my hands. I felt as if all energy was being drained from my being. The very air in my lungs seemed strained. My body began to ache from the pain of exhaustion. All the while, the same words were pouring from my mouth and piercing the air. I no longer controlled the words I spoke. It was beyond my power to influence anything.

I began to hear screams and shouts, gasps and cries. The color vanished from the world, and I was consumed with an overpowering grayness. I was again in the space between the physical and spiritual worlds. The magic was gone from my hands, and I felt like I was floating. It was limbo.

When I looked up, Marilyn was in front of me. She gave me a soft smile before nodding. "I'm ready to come back. It seems you need me, anyway. You've been rather gloomy while I was gone."

I laughed in exasperation. "You have no idea."

In a moment of bright light, she was gone. There were witches all around me. Every few moments, one of them would vanish in what looked like a star exploding. Keeping a connection between the two worlds was causing pain in my chest. I could only do it for so long.

"Esme," my mom whispered.

I looked over to see her standing in a white dress with her brown hair flowing freely around her. Marilyn's mom was there, too. Beside them were two women I didn't recognize. But after looking at them, I knew who they were. One had long, white-blonde hair and pale skin that looked soft as a feather. She was Riona's mother. They could have been mistaken for sisters. The other was tall with chocolate, curly hair and blue eyes I could never misplace. She gave me a gentle smile that told me all I needed to know.

"Take care of my sons," she whispered.

I nodded with a tight smile. "I will."

Riona's mother stepped forward as timidly as a rabbit. "Please tell my daughter I love her, but I won't be coming back. This is her life; mine has passed."

A tear slipped down my cheek. "I'll tell her."

Riona was going to be so disappointed. She had wanted her mom back, but it seemed that wasn't going to happen. How would I explain it to her?

My mom stepped forward. "Oh, Esme. I always knew you were special. Remember, love, you're a queen. Make sure they understand it. Lead our people, and never give up."

With a shaky breath, I replied, "I'll do my best."

She took my hand in hers. "I know."

Marilyn's mom gave me a wave, and I replied with a smile. All of a sudden, it grew quiet. The remaining witches began to fade back into the spiritual realm, and my vision started to grow dark. Then, one more figure materialized.

The girl had bundles of crimson, curly hair, and emerald eyes. She looked up at me with a wide smile on her face. I felt as if my heart had fallen from my chest.

"Mom," she whispered.

I didn't even know what to say. All I could manage was a look of pure astonishment. I'd never expected her to be so gorgeous. She had stolen my heart in less than a second.

"I'll meet you on the other side," Geneva said.

Before I could reply, she disappeared in a flash of light. I was left by myself on the white and black bridge. All of a sudden, my head grew light. My eyes closed, and I fell back into a void of darkness.

CHAPTER TWENTY-ONE
ESME
BACK HOME

The first thing I smelled was the scent of lavender tea drifting through the house. After that came the aroma of sugar cookies and lemon pastries. I heard voices and laughter and felt an overall sense of happiness.

My eyes fluttered open to find Marilyn sitting beside me. I was lying in my bed with candles on the nightstand while she sat next to me with a book open on her lap. Her blonde curls rested around her shoulders. She wore a blue dress and a white cardigan that reminded me of Cinderella. Her pretty pink lips parted in a smile when she saw my open eyes.

"You're awake," she whispered.

I sat up beside her. "Well, bringing you back from the dead was pretty exhausting."

She laughed. "Yes, I expect it was."

I laced her fingers through mine. "How do you feel?"

Her face lit up with light and energy. "I feel perfectly fine. Don't feel even the slightest bit dead."

I laughed. "Well, that's good. I was really missing you. Things got crazy around here."

Marilyn raised her eyebrows. "Oh, I know. It was the best family drama I've ever seen. A wayward sister, an insane, murderous father, and a prophecy about raising the dead. It was the perfect recipe for juicy drama."

I smirked. "Sounds like you didn't mind missing all the excitement. Maybe it was more fun to watch."

She laughed. "Oh, I think it probably was."

Marilyn rested her head against my shoulder. I leaned in against her as she pulled the blanket up around us. For a moment, I didn't think about anything other than the two of us. She was back, and my life felt a little more hopeful. The world seemed less dull. The flowers were sweeter, and the air more open. Even the stars were brighter.

The door began to creak open. My mind suddenly sparked with the realization of the other person who must be in the house. She had been the last thing I had seen before I passed out. Her emerald eyes, almost the same as mine, were brighter than any jewel I had ever glimpsed. When the door slid the rest of the way open, I felt as if I might collapse.

The air seemed to disappear from the room as a gasp escaped my lips. She was standing before me with fiery curls that fell to her hips and thick, ruby lips that were more vibrant than the sweetest strawberry. Her cheeks were scattered with little freckles, and her eyes were full of hope. She wore a dark gray sweater dress that fell past her knees and combat boots with big, heavy socks. I guessed she was maybe fourteen or so. She had grown up without me, but I couldn't have been more stunned at her beauty and how amazing she was.

At that moment, I knew nothing would stop me from reaching my daughter. I hopped off the bed and ran toward her faster than I knew possible. When I finally wrapped my arms around her frail body, she gripped me as though the world were dependent upon our touch. I heard the desperate sobs coursing through my body as I gripped her hair without the slightest intention of letting go.

"Geneva...," I whispered into her red curls.

She rested her head on my shoulder. "I love you so much."

Suddenly, memories began to flash through my mind. This was different than before. They were snippets of my life in 1713. I saw the day she had been born. Her tiny little nose was smaller than my thumb as she rested against me. I heard her pretty little laugh, the way she'd cooed as I smiled at her. The memories flashed through my mind. I saw Sampson holding her and Everest staring at her with a glimmer of happiness in his eyes. It was as if these tiny glimpses of my former life had been unlocked and fallen out of some blocked-off section of my mind. I was amazed at just how much I loved her.

I pulled her even tighter against my chest. "I love you too, baby."

A few moments passed before I sensed Sampson in the doorway. I looked up at him over our daughter's head and smiled. He was staring at me with awe-filled eyes that communicated only one thing, love. I could almost feel his heart beat faster, along with mine. It was a little strange to only appear seventeen and twenty-one when our daughter was fourteen. It didn't matter, though. Having her in my arms was the best thing I had ever experienced.

I pulled away from her to motion toward Marilyn. "Geneva, I assume you've met my best friend, Marilyn."

Geneva nodded. "I met Aunt Mari in the spirit world. She told me I looked like you."

Marilyn smiled. "You sure do."

"And you're both entirely gorgeous," Sampson whispered.

I looked up at him. "I need to speak to Riona."

Sampson led me downstairs to where Everest and Riona sat by the fireplace. Riona's face was streaked with tears, and her icy blonde hair was pulled back in a bun at the back of her head. Her cheeks were flushed, and her lips were puffy and swollen. Everest held his hand on her knee as they sat silently, watching the flames.

Marilyn and Geneva went into the kitchen to retrieve tea. Sampson tapped Everest's shoulder and tilted his head.

After giving me a soft smile and a kiss on my forehead, Everest followed Sampson out of the room. As the brothers walked out, I sat down beside Riona.

She didn't look at me but rather kept her eyes trained on the fire. A single tear slid down her cheek, but she didn't move to brush it away. I didn't feel prepared to handle this. In fact, I wasn't even sure if it was my place. But nevertheless, it was my job.

"Your mother loves you," I whispered.

She held in a sob. "She didn't come back."

I waited a few moments. "She told me to tell you that she loves you. One day, you will see her again. But for now, it's your time to enjoy life."

Riona raised her hands to cover her face. "I have nothing left."

I pulled her against my shoulder. "I know it doesn't feel like much, but you have me and your brothers. You are one of the best friends I've ever had. Whether or not they always show it, I know Sampson and Everest are happy you're their sister. This family needs you. You belong with us."

She rested against me. "I'm sorry I pressured you to bring them back."

I laid my head on top of hers. "It's all right. Besides, the Sages were the ones who threatened to kill the three of you if I didn't agree. What happened to them, anyway?"

"They left after their sister showed up, and you passed

out," she replied.

I shuddered. "I hope we don't see them again."

A small smile crept onto Riona's face. "Nothing like a group of murderous, stereotypical wicked witches to ruin your day."

I shook my head. "Hopefully, their sister is more sane. I'd hate to think I used all my energy to bring another lunatic back into the world."

Riona looked over toward the kitchen, where Geneva was sprinkling brown sugar on a cup of tea. Marilyn was behind her, pulling apples from the pantry. Everest and Sampson were doing their best to avoid them while managing to retrieve a bowl of strawberries. It all looked so average as if we were a normal family.

"You brought Genny back," Riona whispered. "That was reason enough to do it. Even if the world erupts into chaos because of it, I'm glad to have my niece alive. I spoke to Marilyn, too. I think we'll be good friends."

I smiled. "I'm sure you will be. She could probably talk a hungry lion out of eating a lamb. You'll get along great."

"This family...," she whispered, "it's more complicated than I'd imagined. You and my brothers — well, that's something I won't involve myself in. But it only takes a few moments to tell that they love you, and I hope there's some way for all three of you to be happy."

I took her hand in mine before taking a slow, heavy

breath. "I do, too. I just have to figure out how. But today is not the day."

Riona laughed lightly. "You can add that to your list of complicated problems needing answers."

"Yes," I said, "I sure can."

CHAPTER TWENTY-TWO
ESME
QUEEN

The dream came slower this time. As my mind drifted away into an endless sea of relaxation, a sudden silver light invaded the corners of my vision. I sighed; I'd really been hoping the dreams would go away after I fulfilled the prophecy. It seemed like they wouldn't be leaving, though. They appeared to be a permanent part of my new life.

A gentle humming noise startled me out of my contemplation. I turned toward the soft light to see hundreds of witches shrouded in white cloaks, dresses, and robes. As I walked toward them, they created a pathway for me to travel through. They smiled brightly as the familiar sound of a harp began to echo around us. The sheer amount of energy in the air was startling. It gave me a feeling of vibrancy as I continued through the crowd.

Looking down, I noticed a sky-blue dress that was covered in silver sparkles. It was tight around my chest, with a corset that restrained my midsection. Ruffles started at my hips and flowed out until they landed around my feet. It was a beautiful eighteenth-century-style dress that complimented my ample figure. The dress was elegant enough to belong in a ballroom filled with nobility and the glimmer of gold.

White orchids adorned my array of scarlet curls that fell down around me. When I looked at the shiny floor, I could glimpse my reflection. This was far different than the other dreams I'd had. This felt more interactive. It was as if I was participating in the gorgeous event rather than just witnessing or reliving it. This wasn't a memory or a vision. It was real. Like my trips to the bridge between worlds, I was with the spirits.

When I reached the end of the path, I saw my mother, Marilyn's mom, as well as Sampson and Everest's mother, and Riona's mom. They were all smiling at me with proud expressions on their faces. I could tell they were real and not just a figment of my imagination. They were truly with me. Between them stood a tall woman with wavy brown hair that fell to her chest and deep, mahogany eyes. Her cherry lips parted in a wide smile as I approached her. She wore a long, golden dress that fell down to spread out on the ground around her. It was covered in lace with tiny jewels sewn around her chest. Upon her head sat a crown of red roses that made her almost ethereal.

She held a silver crown in her hands adorned with

emeralds and rubies. It was delicate enough to look like a tiara but so pronounced that its superiority couldn't be denied. I shivered at the sight of its beauty.

The woman raised her eyes to the crowd and began to speak. "I, Eula, the first witch in all of history, have the honor of bestowing this crown upon its true owner. For over a millennium, we waited for her first arrival. And after her death, we waited three centuries for her rebirth. Now, she has fulfilled the prophecy that granted our people a new chance at life. Today, she receives the title long believed to be hers."

There was a brief pause as Eula looked down at me. Of course, I had heard many tales about her. She was the ancestor of all witches and warlocks. Without her, none of us would exist. After being granted the gift of magic, she had given birth to three sons and three daughters. Every witch and warlock was alive because of her.

She smiled, giving me a small wink. I bit my lip as anxiety began to run through me. She leaned down to whisper in my ear. "Don't worry, dear. This belongs to you."

I smiled hesitantly before nodding. We made eye contact before she lifted the crown into the air, and it became filled with the sweet aroma of roses as it began to sparkle. All around were tiny butterflies that floated through the gathering. The space was warm but not hot. It held the sensation of a cozy gathering rather than a coronation. We were a family.

Eula looked down at me as she placed the crown on my head. "Cassandra, our queen."

As soon as the crowd started cheering, my vision turned black.

When I woke, it was still dark outside. Light from the moon was pouring through the windows, and two candles were burning on the nightstand. Something had changed, though. A bouquet of golden roses was lying at my bedside next to the candles that hadn't been there before. Along with them was a locket. A simple engraving was carved onto the top—a rosewood tree with wildflowers blooming below. I clicked it open to find a tiny scroll within. After gently pulling it open, I read it.

Her life will bring the final heir,
And carry the burden placed upon her where
She will fight to save her fate and fruit,
But in the end, will be forced to choose.

I rolled the scroll back up and closed it within the locket. It was another prophecy. This was the worst coronation gift I'd ever seen. I had enough doom in my life. After being mystically crowned queen of a worldwide population of witches and warlocks, I had woken up to be greeted with a prophecy predicting my potential downfall. Apparently, I couldn't have even a few hours of restful sleep.

Hearing the rustle of sheets, I turned back around. Geneva was sleeping with her hair sprawled around her, a small smile displayed on her freckle-covered face. I gently ran my hand over her hair and smoothed it down. Her deep sleep appeared restful. Her eyelashes fluttered softly, indicating a peaceful dream. My heart fluttered as I looked at my daughter. Geneva was worth protecting, and I knew my family felt the same.

Everest and Sampson were in the guest room, and Riona was sleeping with Marilyn. Everyone was tired, and I hoped they were having a more restful night than I was. Genny definitely looked content. Watching her sleep, it was hard to ignore the prophecy within the locket sitting on my nightstand. The roses and necklace had clearly been a gift from the spirits. Whether or not I liked what the prophecy said, I was glad to know about it.

It indicated the birth of an heir, but I wasn't sure whether or not that meant Geneva. She was my daughter, but I hadn't conceived or given birth to her in this lifetime. The prophecy was cryptic, and I wasn't sure how to interpret it. Either way, it didn't indicate good things for the child. My crown was heavy enough, and I didn't really want to pass it on. I didn't want Geneva, or a future child, to feel the weight of my responsibility. I wanted her to have the life she didn't get to have three centuries ago. I had missed so much time with her. The last time I had seen her in the physical world, she had only been a baby. Now she was fourteen but still too young to be charged with the burdens I carried. I would, of course, fight to save her, but the prophecy said I would have to choose. If it was a matter of my life or Geneva's, I would want her to live. What kind of mother would I be if I sacrificed her life for my own?

I wanted to be able to enjoy life with her. I wanted us to be a normal, happy family. The fact that I had feelings for both men in the next room over didn't help make our situation more average, but it was one thing I could deal with. The gloom and doom warnings only heightened my anxiety. It weighed me down, but I couldn't abandon it. Thousands of witches had entrusted me with the honor of leading them. Whether or not I wanted to do it didn't really matter. Being their queen was my responsibility. I would do my best every day and try to keep them safe.

Laying back down, I pulled the blanket around Geneva and tucked her in. When I situated myself on the pillow, I turned to watch her sleep. As I felt the exhaustion begin to pull me back down, I realized there was nothing more calming than the sight of my daughter's face.

CHAPTER TWENTY-THREE
ESME
POISON AND PETUNIAS

The sun had only begun to rise when I woke. Geneva was still asleep beside me. I could see her torso's gentle rise and fall as she breathed. For a moment, I watched her. My focus was trapped by the frailness of her young teenage body. My physical form was only three years older than hers, but it might as well have been twenty. From what I had learned, time was about much more than calendar days. Age wasn't something that could be correctly interpreted from a simple guess. I no longer knew what to think of time. But I wouldn't worry about it—yet. One day when I had finished slaying the last of my metaphorical dragons, I could think about the meaning of age. For now, I would simply treasure the image of my daughter.

But while I watched her sleep, thoughts of how much I had missed ran through my mind. I had no baby pictures of her. I had missed the first day she walked, the first word she spoke, and the first fairytale she'd heard. After she died as an infant, all her growth had occurred in some metaphysical, time-slowing spiritual slumber. Now she was here as a fourteen-year-old innocent girl, and I had no clue what to do. How was I, a seventeen-year-old, supposed to parent my daughter from a previous life? I loved her, and I wanted to make sure she was safe, but I just didn't think I would be good enough at being her mother. Yes, I had a few glimpses from the past. Those memories were so, so valuable. I'd inherited a lot of things from my years as Cassandra, but my daughter was the most complicated and gorgeous part of my continued life.

Sampson was more confident than me. He had jumped into father duty like it was as natural as walking. It seemed like second nature to him. He had already spent hours teaching her spells. They got along so well that it seemed they'd spent years together. Geneva already looked up to him, and he appeared ready for the responsibility. When comparing myself to him, I felt like a goose pretending to be a swan. My parenting abilities had not yet reached Sampson's level of natural expertise.

Marilyn seemed completely adjusted to the idea that I had a daughter. She treated Geneva like her niece and acted like the cool, relaxed aunt everyone thought of as their second-best friend. I was glad they liked each other. Geneva seemed completely content with her long-lost family.

Everest looked at her with curiosity. He seemed too hesitant to want to talk to her but too fascinated to ignore her presence. I had a feeling he didn't know what to say. The fact that I was currently stuck between her father and uncle didn't make me anxious to explain our dynamic to Geneva. I didn't know how to make sense of it, no less make it sound sane.

Riona had been distant since her mother had declined to come back. She knew the reasons, but she was still surprised and upset. I wanted to comfort her, but there wasn't much I could say. Geneva was the only one who seemed to be able to brighten her depressed mood. When Geneva approached, Riona looked at her as if she was the world's hope. And maybe she was—maybe Geneva was our hope. She was bright, kind, and happy. I didn't want to dim her light. Geneva was like a flame that had only just begun to burn but was literally glowing with potential. She made me want to fight, and perhaps that said more about me as a mother than the other things did. Maybe my desire to protect her was enough for the moment. She was a cub, and I would be her lioness.

I slid out of bed before tucking her back under the covers. She hadn't even moved. I smiled softly as I brushed her hair out of her face. This would be her first morning on earth since the day our lives had ended three hundred years ago. At least this was one first I would be able to be a part of.

I pulled my nightgown off in exchange for a woolen dress. It was a dark color that reminded me of evergreen trees during a light snow. I brushed my hair and let it fall across my shoulders as I pulled the top section back into a bun. After wrapping a white shawl around my body, I examined myself in the mirror.

I touched my ruby curls that fell down around mein a hurricane of frizz. My eyes were still light and galaxy-like, but there was a different level of understanding. I was tired from the battles I had fought and stressed about the future. Somehow I looked older than I had a week ago and felt like it too. After the things I had experienced, I no longer felt seventeen. The world was different, as was my perception of it. I had discovered more about myself and was becoming the person I was supposed to be. This new version of myself was strong, and I was proud of her. But I was exhausted, too.

Not wanting to wake Genny, I walked carefully down the hall. When I reached the steps, I moved as softly as I could. I wanted to be able to make coffee without waking anyone. But when I reached the main floor, Everest was already sitting at the kitchen table.

He smiled at me when I approached. "I thought you were up." He handed me a mug of coffee before motioning for me to sit with him. "How did you sleep?"

I took a sip. "Fine, just another dream." I wasn't going to tell any of them about the prophecy. They didn't need to worry over something I didn't understand. Maybe one day I could tell them.

He smiled. "Sounds like another typical night for you."

Everest slipped his hand into mine and intertwined our fingers. I allowed him to do so without protest. There was no doubt that I wanted to be with him. When he had come to find me in the hills, we had felt a beautiful moment of passionate bliss. I wanted Everest, but I also wanted Sampson. It didn't feel right to love them both at once, but I couldn't really stop myself. Whenever one of them reached for me, I reached back. There was so much pent-up love inside my heart and such a deep connection to both of them that I could hardly stop myself. I would have to choose, but not yet. For now, we seemed content with being a complicated, temporary triad. It would end, and one of them would probably move on to someone else, but I had a little time.

Everest brought my fingers to his lips and kissed them. They were tender and gentle. Everything about him was romantic. He was a genuine Romeo. Everest was the perfect Mr. Right, but there was something about Sampson, some alluring aspect that drew my heart toward him. Everest was the cool, beautiful ocean, and Sampson was the waves crashing toward the earth. There was something in me that adored both of them. I closed my eyes as Everest released my hand. When I opened them, he was glancing at me worriedly.

"What's wrong?" Everest asked gently.

I looked down. "I still don't know."

He smiled before brushing my hair aside. "I know,

but my feelings for you will stay the same. There's no getting past you, Esme. Ignoring you would be like trying to live without the sun. I wouldn't feel truly alive if you weren't in my life. From the moment we made eye contact in the forest, I knew I had met the most beautiful woman I would ever see. I saw a star blazing in your heart, and I knew I couldn't turn away. Now that I've learned about our past, I understand my feelings. My love for you is clear and open. We were together as Clovis and Cassandra, and I hope we will be again. But I'll wait for you as long as it takes, and I'm not backing down."

"I don't want to prevent you from finding a less complicated relationship," I whispered.

He took my face in his hands. "Esme, you are the most important person, other than Sampson, in my life. No matter who you choose, I'll be here if you change your mind."

He leaned over to place a soft kiss on my lips. I tasted the coffee he had been drinking and the leftover strawberry from the jam he'd had on his muffin. His lips were as soft as cream. He was persistent and gentle, somehow making a sweet combination of the two. Heat began to bubble up within me as he wrapped his arm around my back. He pulled me closer and laced his fingers in my curls. I let my hands travel to his long hair tied back at the nape of his neck. Everest was addictive, and I couldn't get enough of the way his lips pressed against mine.

All of a sudden, I was on the floor. Everest had thrown

his body over mine to protect me from the shattered glass that had flown toward us. The whole window had erupted. It all happened so quickly that I'd barely known what was happening. There was an arrow notched into the chair I had been sitting in only seconds ago. It had been aimed at my heart.

Everest stood and pulled the arrow out of the chair. It was metal and dripping with elderberry juice. If it had pierced my chest, I would have been poisoned. Combined with the toxic nature of the juices and the blood I would have lost, I would have died. The arrow had been meant to kill me.

Sampson thundered down the stairs with Marilyn, Riona, and Geneva right behind. They all had terrified expressions on their faces. When Sampson saw the arrow, anger clouded his features.

"What happened?" Sampson asked.

"Someone shot this at her heart," Everest answered.

Riona gasped. "There's poison on it."

Marilyn pursed her lips before traveling over to the shattered window. Muttering a quick repair spell, she caused the glass to rise back up into its original place. Once making sure the window was secure and in one piece, she pulled the curtains shut. Marilyn proceeded to walk around the first floor, locking all of the windows. After all the curtains were closed, Riona lit a few candles. Geneva stood beside Sampson in stunned silence.

Everest wiped all the elderberry off the arrow before taking a closer look. When he could see it clearly, he turned toward me. His eyes were filled with fear and worry.

"What is it?" Sampson asked.

Everest handed the arrow to him. I watched while Sampson examined the tool meant to cause my death. I was still so shocked that I couldn't think of much to say. Geneva stayed at Sampson's side with a scared expression on her face. Anger began to build up within me. I didn't want her involved in this. Geneva had already died once because of the actions of an evil, homicidal maniac. I didn't want her to relive any of the trauma she'd experienced three hundred years ago. This was meant to be different; I wanted to keep her safe.

Sampson looked directly at Everest. "It says, 'You're next.'"

Riona raised her eyebrows. "Assassination attempts are disturbingly prevalent around here."

Sampson passed the arrow to her. "Well, the fact that thousands of age-old witches, some of whom clearly have grudges against our family, just came back from the dead isn't helping the situation."

"I thought it was over," Geneva whispered. "Why would witches and warlocks fight each other? We spent so long trying to protect ourselves from the humans, and now we're trying to kill our own people?"

"It appears so," Marilyn said. "Some of these witches

clearly have problems with us, but we don't even know why they're angry. We have no idea who's coming after us."

"We have to focus on keeping everyone safe," Everest said. "Until we know who tried to kill Esme, we have to be cautious."

I looked between all of them. Sampson had his arms crossed and a protective glint in his eyes. His dark hair was still messy from sleep, making him look accidentally handsome. Geneva was standing beside him with a solemn expression on her young, clear face. Riona and Marilyn stood off to the side. They were both looking at me with a mixture of stress and support. I could see the fear on their faces, but also passion. We would protect each other. Everest was beside me with a contemplative look on his face. His blue eyes were focused off in the distance while stressful thoughts occupied his mind.

As the most powerful witch of all time, I should have been able to protect them. They were my best friends — my family. I didn't feel strong. It was as if the weight of my people had been placed on my shoulders. On top of leading them, I had somehow amassed enemies. Someone was trying to kill me, and that put the people I loved at risk. It endangered my daughter. Whoever was trying to hurt me clearly wanted my family dead, too. But when we found out who the would-be-assassin was, we would do what was necessary to protect our family. I wouldn't let anyone hurt them. There was power in me I had yet to realize. I hadn't learned how to pull from its energy, but I would. When I wasn't fighting the dangers sent our way, I would learn how to use my magic. If I was going to be faced with the dangers of my past, I had to accept my identity. This was a task fit for Cassandra—a queen—and it was time I learned to rule.

CHAPTER TWENTY-FOUR
ESME
THE SUN STILL BURNS

The fire blazed brightly as I watched the flames sizzle. I had always found a certain fascination within the flames. Something about the elegance of the fire sparked my interest. There was such a naturalness to it but also a sense of magic. The fire didn't struggle to control its power. It simply burned. There wasn't hesitation or anxiety. Fire didn't worry about the perception of the birds. It was powerful and confident. The natural strength was deserving of respect.

I envied the flames. They were confident, while I felt unsure. No matter how much I did, I wasn't positive of my abilities. I had literally brought thousands of witches back to life, including my best friend and daughter, but I still felt weak. Being Cassandra was harder than I had expected. No one else seemed to understand the weight. My crown felt like a thousand diamonds pushing down to squish me into the ground.

I had been poring over spell books, searching through old documents, and working to live up to my name. I didn't want power to abuse it. I wanted the ability to protect my family and do my job. The spirits had given me a gift, and I was responsible for leading my people. I wanted to be able to do the harder spells. I was supposed to be able to do marvelous things. Some of the thicker books held the most complex spells I had ever heard of. I needed to master my ability to control my magic, harness my energy, and use my talents. I had more sheer power than any other witch. I simply had to learn how to use it. If I could complete the harder spells, I would be able to heal the sick, hold back fire, and cause tremendous pain with a single glance. I could protect my daughter; that was enough motivation to keep me awake after midnight, practicing until I was capable of unbelievable feats.

Geneva was sitting beside Marilyn, who was teaching her a new recipe. They were both crushing berries before tossing them into the pot above the fire. Riona was sitting close to them as she sharpened her arrows. In the moonlight, their faces were shining. I smiled softly as I watched them. My heart felt light when I saw their joy.

Sampson was sitting on my right. His hair was still wet from his shower, and his eyes were bright with admiration as he looked at Geneva. There was so much love in his eyes. I knew he would do anything to protect our daughter. It was enough to make me look at him as a man with great resilience. There was passion for him in my heart. We were so alike.

Everest was on my left. He was sipping a cup of tea while staring into the flames. I wondered what he was thinking. Would he share it with me? It had been three days since the attack, and he had been quiet ever since. There was beauty in his contemplation. I didn't want to disturb his thoughts.

This was the way I wanted it to be. I was between them, and I loved having both of them with me. They were the two most important men in my life. I adored both of them. And yes, I wanted to love both of them at the same time. But I couldn't. They each deserved someone who would love them exclusively for their whole lives. I wouldn't choose tonight, though.

"This family is going to become legendary," Sampson whispered.

I hadn't told either of them about the prophecy within the locket around my neck. The spirits had given it to me, but I didn't want to tell anyone yet. Geneva didn't deserve to have that on her. For now, it was a warning. But my daughter would be phenomenal. I was certain of that.

"I know," I replied.

Everest looked at both of us with a glimmer of happiness in his eyes. I smiled back at him. We shared a small glance filled with love.

Sampson gave his brother a happy grin. "There's a fight coming," Sampson said. "But we'll win because we have more to fight for."

I looked back at Geneva. "If they try to hurt her, they will suffer."

Sampson nodded. "Agreed."

"And when they come for you," Everest said, "they'll learn just how strong a queen can be."

Later that night, I rested in my bed. The moon had come out from behind the clouds. As I looked at the dark ceiling illuminated by candlelight, I couldn't tear my thoughts away from the reality that I was the most powerful witch in history and wholly in love with two brothers who had taken my heart.

Books Currently Available by Abby Farnsworth

EverGreen Trilogy

The Shades of Us Trilogy

Abby Farnsworth is an award-winning Young Adult Paranormal Romance and Fantasy Author. Abby enjoys writing about a wide variety of characters within the Paranormal Romance and Fantasy genres, including faeries, vampires, witches, and werewolves. Her novels are all centered around romance, but also feature adventure and suspense. Her first novel, *EverGreen*, received the Literary Titan Silver Star Award, and her second and third novels, *Moonlit Skies* and *Fallen Snow*, received the Literary Titan Gold Star Award.

Abby currently resides in West Virginia, and enjoys reading, nature, and long walks.

To learn more about Abby, her books, and current projects, take a look at the following:
#authorabbyfarnsworth
#theevergreentrilogy
Instagram: @abbyfarnsworth.writer
Facebook: @abbyfarnsworth.writer.poet

www.ingramcontent.com/pod-product-compliance
Lightning Source LLC
Chambersburg PA
CBHW030334180626
46810CB00003B/1346